THE SUNNY SIDE

THE SUNNY SIDE

A. A. MILNE

ISIS
LARGE PRINT
Oxford

Copyright © A. A. Milne, 1921

First published in Great Britain 1921
by
Methuen & Co Ltd.

Published in Large Print 2006 by ISIS Publishing Ltd.,
7 Centremead, Osney Mead, Oxford OX2 0ES
by arrangement with
Snowbooks Ltd.

British Library Cataloguing in Publication Data
Milne, A. A. (Alan Alexander), 1882–1956
    The sunny side.– Large print ed.
    1. Large type books
    I. Title
    823.9'12 [F]

            ISBN 0–7531–7608–4 (hb)
            ISBN 0–7531–7609–2 (pb)

Printed and bound in Great Britain by
T. J. International Ltd., Padstow, Cornwall

To Owen Seaman

Affectionately In Memory Of Nine
Happy Years At The "Punch" Office

Contents

Introduction

My publisher wants me to apologize for — "introduce" was the kindly word he used — this collection of articles and verses from *Punch*. I do so with pleasure.

Among the many interests of a long and varied career —

No, I don't think I shall begin like that.

It was early in 1871 —

Nor like that.

Really it is very difficult, you know. I wrote these things for a number of years, and — well, here they are. But just to say "Here they are" is to be too informal for my publisher. He wants, not a casual introduction, but a presentation. Let me tell you a little story instead.

When war broke out, I had published three of these books in England, the gleanings of nine years' regular work for *Punch*. There are, I understand, a few Americans who read *Punch*, and it was suggested to me that a suitable collection of articles from these three books might have some sort of American sale. So I made such a collection, leaving out the more topical and allusive sketches, and including those with a more general appeal. I called the result "Happy Days" — an attractive title, you will agree — and in 1915 a New York publisher was found for it.

This is a funny story; at least it appeals to *me*; so I won't remind myself of the number of copies which we sold. That was tragedy, not comedy. The joke lay in one of the few notices which the book received from the press. For a New York critic ended his review of "Happy Days" with these immortal words:

"Mr. Milne is at present in the trenches facing the German bullets, so this will probably be his last book."

You see now why an apology is necessary. Here we are, seven years later, and I am still at it.

But at any rate, it is the last of this sort of book. As I said in a foreword to the English edition: "It is the last time because this sort of writing depends largely upon the irresponsibility and high spirits of youth for its success, and I want to stop before (may I say 'before'?) the high spirits become mechanical and the irresponsibility a trick. Perhaps the fact that this collection is final will excuse its air of scrappiness. Odd Verses have crept in on the unanswerable plea that, if they didn't do it now, they never would; War Sketches protested that I shouldn't have a book at all if I left them out; an Early Article, omitted from three previous volumes, paraded for the fourth time with such a pathetic 'I suppose you don't want *me*' in its eye that it could not decently be rejected. So here they all are."

One further word of explanation. You may find the first section of this book — "Oranges and Lemons" — a little difficult. The characters of it are old friends to that limited public which reads my books in England; their earlier adventures have been told in those previous volumes (and purposely omitted from "Happy Days" as being a little too insular). I feel somehow that strangers will not be on such easy terms with them, and I would recommend that you approach them last. By that time you will have discovered whether you are in a mood to stop and listen to their chatter, or prefer to pass them by with a nod.

A. A. M.

Oranges and Lemons

I. THE INVITATION

"Dear Myra," wrote Simpson at the beginning of the year — "I have an important suggestion to make to you both, and I am coming round tomorrow night after dinner about nine o'clock. As time is so short I have asked Dahlia and Archie to meet me there, and if by any chance you have gone out we shall wait till you come back.

"Yours ever,

"SAMUEL

"P.S. — I have asked Thomas too."

"Well?" said Myra eagerly, as I gave her back the letter.

In deep thought I buttered a piece of toast.

"We could stop Thomas," I said. "We might ring up the Admiralty and ask them to give him something to do this evening. I don't know about Archie. Is he —"

"Oh, what do you think it is? Aren't you excited?" She sighed and added, "Of course I know what Samuel is."

"Yes. Probably he wants us all to go to the Zoo together . . . or he's discovered a new way of putting, or — I say, I didn't know Archie and Dahlia were in town."

"They aren't. But I expect Samuel telegraphed to them to meet him under the clock at Charing Cross disguised, when they would hear of something to their advantage. Oh, I wonder what it is. It *must* be something real this time."

Since the day when Simpson woke me up at six o'clock in the morning to show me his stance-for-a-full-wooden-club shot, I have distrusted his enthusiasms; but Myra loves him as a mother; and I — I couldn't do without him; and when a man like that invites a whole crowd of people to come to your flat just about the time when you are wondering what has happened to the sardines on toast — well, it isn't polite to put the chain on the door and explain through the letter-box that you have gone away for a week.

"We'd better have dinner a bit earlier to be on the safe side," I said, as Myra gave me a parting brush down in the hall. "If any further developments occur in the course of the day, ring me up at the office. By the way, Simpson doesn't seem to have invited Peter. I wonder why not. He's nearly two, and he ought to be in it. Myra, I'm sure I'm tidy now."

"Pipe, tobacco, matches, keys, money?"

"Everything," I said. "Bless you. Goodbye."

"Good-bye," said Myra lingeringly. "What do you think he meant by 'as time is so short'?"

"I don't know. At least," I added, looking at my watch, "I do know I shall be horribly late. Good-bye."

I fled down the stairs into the street, waved to Myra at the window . . . and then came cautiously up again for my pipe. Life is very difficult on the mornings when you are in a hurry.

At dinner that night Myra could hardly eat for excitement.

"You'll be sorry afterwards," I warned her, "when it turns out to be nothing more than that he has had his hair cut."

"But even if it is, I don't see why I shouldn't be excited at seeing my only brother again — not to mention sister-in-law."

"Then let's move," I said. "They'll be here directly."

Archie and Dahlia came first. We besieged them with questions as soon as they appeared.

"Haven't an idea," said Archie, "I wanted to bring a revolver in case it was anything really desperate, but Dahlia wouldn't let me."

"It would have been useful too," I said, "if it turned out to be something merely futile."

"You're not going to hurt my Samuel, however futile it is," said Myra. "Dahlia, how's Peter, and will you have some coffee?"

"Peter's lovely. You've had coffee, haven't you, Archie?"

"Better have some more," I suggested, "in case Simpson is merely soporific. We anticipate a slumbering audience, and Samuel explaining a new kind of googlie he's invented."

Entered Thomas lazily.

"Hallo," he said in his slow voice. "What's it all about?"

"It's a raid on the Begum's palace," explained Archie rapidly. "Dahlia decoys the Chief Mucilage; you, Thomas, drive the submarine; Myra has charge of the clockwork mouse, and we others hang about and sing. To say more at this stage would be to bring about a European conflict."

"Coffee, Thomas?" said Myra.

"I bet he's having us on," said Thomas gloomily, as he stirred his coffee.

There was a hurricane in the hall. Chairs were swept over; coats and hats fell to the ground; a high voice offered continuous apologies — and Simpson came in.

"Hallo, Myra!" he said eagerly. "Hallo, old chap! Hallo, Dahlia! Hallo, Archie! Hallo, Thomas, old boy!" He fixed his spectacles firmly on his nose and beamed round the room.

"We're all here — thanking you very much for inviting us," I said. "Have a cigar — if you've brought any with you."

Fortunately he had brought several with him.

"Now then, I'll give any of you three guesses what it's all about."

"No, you don't. We're all waiting, and you can begin your apology right away."

Simpson took a deep breath and began.

"I've been lent a villa," he said.

There was a moment's silence . . . and then Archie got up.

"Good-bye," he said to Myra, holding out his hand. "Thanks for a very jolly evening. Come along Dahlia."

"But I say, old chap," protested Simpson.

"I'm sorry, Simpson, but the fact that you're moving from the Temple to Cricklewood, or wherever it is, and that somebody else is paying the thirty pounds a year, is jolly interesting, but it wasn't good enough to drag us up from the country to tell us about it. You could have written. However, thank you for the cigar."

"My dear fellow, it isn't Cricklewood. It's the Riviera!"

Archie sat down again.

"Samuel!" cried Myra. "How she must love you!"

"I should never lend Simpson a villa of mine," I said. "He'd only lose it."

"They're some very old friends who live there, and they're going away for a month, and the servants are staying on, and they suggested that if I was going abroad again this year —"

"How did the servants know you'd been abroad last year?" asked Archie.

"Don't interrupt, dear," said Dahlia. "I see what he means. How very jolly for you, Samuel."

"For all of us, Dahlia!"

"You aren't suggesting we shall all crowd in?" growled Thomas.

"Of course, my dear old chap! I told them, and they're delighted. We can share housekeeping expenses, and it will be as cheap as anything."

"But to go into a stranger's house," said Dahlia anxiously.

"It's *my* house, Dahlia, for the time. I invite you!" He threw out his hands in a large gesture of welcome and knocked his coffee-cup on to the carpet, begged Myra's pardon several times and then sat down again and wiped his spectacles vigorously.

Archie looked doubtfully at Thomas.

"Duty, Thomas, duty," he said, thumping his chest. "You can't desert the Navy at this moment of crisis."

"Might," said Thomas, puffing at his pipe.

Archie looked at me. I looked hopefully at Myra.

"Oh-h-h!" said Myra, entranced.

Archie looked at Dahlia. Dahlia frowned.

"It isn't till February," said Simpson eagerly.

"It's very kind of you, Samuel," said Dahlia, "but I don't think —"

Archie nodded to Simpson.

"You leave this to me," he said confidentially. "We're going."

II. ON THE WAY

"Toulon," announced Archie, as the train came to a stop and gave out its plaintive, dying whistle. "Naval port of our dear allies, the French. This would interest Thomas."

"If he weren't asleep," I said.

"He'll be here directly," said Simpson from the little table for two on the other side of the gangway. "I'm afraid he had a bad night. Here, *garçon* — er — *donnez-moi du café et* — er —" But the waiter had slipped past him again — the fifth time.

"Have some of ours," said Myra kindly, holding out the pot.

"Thanks very much, Myra, but I may as well wait for Thomas, and — *garçon, du café pour* — I don't think he'll be — *deux cafés, garçon, s'il vous* — it's going to be a lovely day."

Thomas came in quietly, sat down opposite Simpson, and ordered breakfast.

"Samuel wants some too," said Myra.

Thomas looked surprised, grunted and ordered another breakfast.

"You see how easy it is," said Archie. "Thomas, we're at Toulon, where the *ententes cordiales* come from. You ought to have been up long ago taking notes for the Admiralty."

"I had a rotten night," said Thomas. "Simpson fell out of bed in the middle of it."

"Oh, poor Samuel!"

"You don't mean to say you gave him the top berth?" I asked in surprise. "You must have known he'd fall out."

"But, Thomas dear, surely Samuel's just falling-out-of-bed noise wouldn't wake you up," said Myra. "I always thought you slept so well."

"He tried to get back into *my* bed."

"I was a little dazed," explained Simpson hastily, "and I hadn't got my spectacles."

"Still you ought to have been able to see Thomas there."

"Of course I did see him as soon as I got in, and then I remembered I was up above. So I climbed up."

"It must be rather difficult climbing up at night," thought Dahlia.

"Not if you get a good take-off, Dahlia," said Simpson earnestly.

"Simpson got a good one off my face," explained Thomas.

"My dear old chap, I was frightfully sorry. I did come down at once and tell you how sorry I was, didn't I?"

"You stepped back on to it," said Thomas shortly, and he turned his attention to the coffee.

Our table had finished breakfast. Dahlia and Myra got up slowly, and Archie and I filled our pipes and followed them out.

"Well, we'll leave you to it," said Archie to the other table.

"Personally, I think it's Thomas's turn to step on Simpson. But don't be long, because there's a good view coming."

The good view came, and then another and another, and they merged together and became one long, moving panorama of beauty. We stood in the corridor and drank it in . . . and at intervals we said "Oh-h!" and "Oh, I say!" and "Oh, I say, *really*!" And there was one particular spot I wish I could remember where, so that it might be marked by a suitable tablet — at the sight of which Simpson was overheard to say, "*Mon Dieu!*" for (probably) the first time in his life.

"You know, all these are olive trees, you chaps," he said every five minutes. "I wonder if there are any olives growing on them?"

"Too early," said Archie. "It's the sardine season now."

It was at Cannes that we saw the first oranges.

"That does it," I said to Myra. "We're really here. And look, there's a lemon tree. Give me the oranges and lemons, and you can have all the palms and the cactuses and the olives."

"Like polar bears in the arctic regions," said Myra.

I thought for a moment. Superficially there is very little resemblance between an orange and a polar bear.

"Like polar bears," I said hopefully.

"I mean," luckily she went on, "polar bears do it for you in the polar regions. You really know you're there then. Give me the polar bears, I always say, and you can keep the seals and the walruses and the penguins. It's the hallmark."

"Right. I knew you meant something. In London," I went on, "it is raining. Looking out of my window I see a lamp-post (not in flower) beneath a low, grey sky.

Here we see oranges against a blue sky a million miles deep. What a blend! Myra, let's go to a fancy-dress ball when we get back. You go as an orange and I'll go as a very blue, blue sky, and you shall lean against me."

"And we'll dance the tangerine," said Myra.

But now observe us approaching Monte Carlo. For an hour past Simpson has been collecting his belongings. Two bags, two coats, a camera, a rug, Thomas, golf-clubs, books — his compartment is full of things which have to be kept under his eye lest they should evade him at the last moment. As the train leaves Monaco his excitement is intense.

"I think, old chap," he says to Thomas, "I'll wear the coats after all."

"And the bags," says Thomas, "and then you'll have a suit."

Simpson puts on the two coats and appears very big and hot.

"I'd better have my hands free," he says, and straps the camera and the golf-clubs on to himself. "Then if you nip out and get a porter I can hand the bags out to him through the window."

"All right," says Thomas. He is deep in his book and looks as if he were settled in his corner of the carriage for the day.

The train stops. There is bustle, noise, confusion. Thomas in some magical way has disappeared. A porter appears at the open window and speaks voluble French to Simpson. Simpson looks round wildly for Thomas. "Thomas!" he cries. "*Un moment*," he says to the porter. "Thomas! *Mon ami, it n'est pas* — I say,

14

Thomas, old chap, where are you? *Attendez un moment. Mon ami — er — reviendra —*" He is very hot. He is wearing, in addition to what one doesn't mention, an ordinary waistcoat, a woolly waistcoat for steamer use, a tweed coat, an aquascutum, an ulster, a camera and a bag of golf clubs. The porter, with many gesticulations, is still hurling French at him.

It is too much for Simpson. He puts his head out of the window and, observing in the distance a figure of such immense dignity that it can only belong to the station-master, utters to him across the hurly-burly a wild call for help.

"*Ou est Cooks's homme?*" he cries.

III. SETTLING DOWN

The villa was high up on the hill, having (as Simpson was to point out several times later) Mentone on its left hand and Monte Carlo on its right. A long winding path led up through its garden of olives to the front door, and through the mimosa trees which flanked this door we could see already a flutter of white aprons. The staff was on the loggia waiting to greet us.

We halted a moment out of sight of the ladies above and considered ourselves. It came to us with a sudden shock that we were a very large party.

"I suppose," said Archie to Simpson, "they do expect all of us and not only you? You told them that about half London was coming?"

"We're only six," said Myra, "because I've just counted again, but we seem about twenty."

"It's quite all right," said Simpson cheerfully. "I said we'd be six."

"But six in a letter is much smaller than six of us like this; and when they see our luggage —

"Let's go back," I suggested, suddenly nervous. To be five guests of the guest of a man you have never met is delicate work.

At this critical moment Archie assumed command. He is a Captain in the Yeomanry and has tackled bigger jobs than this in his time.

"We must get ourselves into proper order," he said. "Simpson, the villa has been lent to *you*; you must go first. Dahlia and I come next. When we arrive you will introduce us as your friends, Mr. and Mrs. Mannering.

Then turning to Myra you say, 'Mr. Mannering's sister; and this,' you add, 'is her husband.' Then — er — Thomas —"

"It will be difficult to account for Thomas," I said. "Thomas comes at the end. He hangs back a little at first; and then if he sees that there is going to be any awkwardness about him, he can pretend he's come on the wrong night, and apologize and go home again."

"If Thomas goes, I go," said Myra dramatically.

"I have another idea," I said. "Thomas hides here for a bit. We introduce ourselves and settle in, and have lunch; and after lunch we take a stroll in the garden, and to our great surprise discover Thomas. 'Thomas,' we say, 'you here? Dear old chap, we thought you were in England. How splendid! Where are you staying? Oh, but you must stop with us; we can easily have a bed put up for you in the garage.' And then —"

"Not after lunch," said Thomas; "before lunch."

"Don't all be so silly," smiled Dahlia. "They'll wonder what has happened to us if we wait any longer. Besides, the men will be here with the luggage directly. Come along."

"Samuel," said Archie, "forward."

In our new formation we marched up, Simpson excited and rehearsing to himself the words of introduction, we others outwardly calm. At a range of ten yards he opened fire. "How do you do?" he beamed. "Here we all are! Isn't it a lovely —"

The cook-housekeeper, majestic but kindly, came forward with outstretched hand and welcomed him volubly — in French. The other three ladies added their

French to hers. There was only one English body on the loggia. It belonged to a bull-dog. The bull-dog barked loudly at Simpson in English.

There was no "Cook's homme" to save Simpson this time. But he rose to the occasion nobly. The scent of the mimosa inspired him.

"*Merci*," he said, "*merci. Oui, n'est ce pas!* Delightful. Er — these are — *ces sont mes amis.* Er — Dahlia, come along — er, *Monsieur et Madame Mannering* — er — Myra, *la soeur de Monsieur* — er — where are you, old chap? — *le mari de la soeur de Monsieur.* Er — Thomas — er —" (he was carried away by memories of his schoolboy French), "*le frère du jardinier* — er —" He wheeled round and saw me; introduced me again; introduced Myra as my wife, Archie as her brother, and Dahlia as Archie's wife; and then with a sudden inspiration presented Thomas grandly as "*le beau-père du petit fils de mes amis Monsieur et Madame Mannering.*" Thomas seemed more assured of his place as Peter's godfather than as the brother of the gardener.

There were four ladies; we shook hands with all of them. It took us a long time, and I doubt if we got it all in even so, for twice I found myself shaking hands with Simpson. But these may have been additional ones thrown in. It was over at last, and we followed the staff indoors.

And then we had another surprise. It was broken to us by Dahlia, who, at Simpson's urgent request, took up the position of lady of the house, and forthwith received the flowing confidences of the housekeeper.

18

"Two of us have to sleep outside," she said.

"Where?" we all asked blankly.

We went on to the loggia again, and she pointed to a little house almost hidden by olive-trees in a corner of the garden below us.

"Oh, well, that's all right," said Archie. "It's on the estate. Thomas, you and Simpson won't mind that a bit, will you?"

"We can't turn Samuel out of his own house," said Myra indignantly.

"We aren't turning him; he wants to go. But, of course, if you and your young man would like to live there instead —"

Myra looked at me eagerly.

"It would be rather fun," she said. "We'd have another little honeymoon all to ourselves."

"It wouldn't really be a honeymoon," I objected. "We should always be knocking up against trippers in the garden, Archies and Samuels and Thomases and what not. They'd be all over the place."

Dahlia explained the domestic arrangements. The honeymooners had their little breakfast in their own little house, and then joined the others for the day at about ten.

"Or eleven," said Thomas.

"It would be rather lovely," said Myra thoughtfully.

"Yes," I agreed; "but have you considered that — Come over this way a moment, where Thomas and Simpson can't hear, while I tell you some of the disadvantages."

I led her into a quiet corner and suggested a few things to her which I hoped would not occur to the other two.

Item: That if it was raining hard at night, it would be beastly.

Item: That if you suddenly found you'd left your pipe behind, it would be rotten.

Item: That if, as was probable, there wasn't a proper bathroom in the little house, it would be sickening.

Item: That if she had to walk on muddy paths in her evening shoes, it would be —

At this point Myra suddenly caught the thread of the argument. We went back to the others.

"We think," said Myra, "it would be perfectly heavenly in the little house; but —" She hesitated.

"But at the same time," I said, "we think it's up to Simpson and Thomas to be English gentlemen. Samuel, it's your honour."

There was a moment's silence.

"Come along," said Thomas to Simpson, "let's go and look at it."

After lunch, clean and well-fed and happy, we lay in deck-chairs on the loggia and looked lazily down at the Mediterranean.

"Thank you, Samuel, for bringing us," said Dahlia gently. "Your friends must be very fond of you to have lent you this lovely place."

"Not fonder than we are," said Myra, smiling at him.

IV. BEFORE LUNCH

I found Myra in the hammock at the end of the loggia.

"Hallo," I said.

"Hallo." She looked up from her book and waved her hand. "Mentone on the left, Monte Carlo on the right," she said, and returned to her book again. Simpson had mentioned the situation so many times that it had become a catch-phrase with us.

"Fancy reading on a lovely morning like this," I complained.

"But that's why. It's a very gloomy play by Ibsen, and whenever it's simply more than I can bear, I look up and see Mentone on the left, Monte Carlo on the right — I mean, I see all the loveliness round me, and then I know the world isn't so bad after all." She put her book down. "Are you alone?"

I gripped her wrist suddenly and put the paper-knife to her throat.

"We are alone," I hissed — or whatever you do to a sentence without any "s"s in it to make it dramatic. "Your friends cannot save you now. Prepare to — er — come walk up the hill with me."

"Help! Help!" whispered Myra. She hesitated a moment; then swung herself out of the hammock and went in for her hat.

We climbed up a steep path which led to the rock-village above us. Simpson had told us that we must see the village; still more earnestly he had begged us to see Corsica. The view of Corsica was to be obtained from a point some miles up — too far to go before lunch.

"However, we can always say we saw it," I reassured Myra. "From this distance you can't be certain of recognizing an island you don't know. Any small cloud on the horizon will do."

"I know it on the map."

"Yes, but it looks quite different in real life. The great thing is to be able to assure Simpson at lunch that the Corsican question is now closed. When we're a little higher up, I shall say, 'Surely that's Corsica?' and you'll say, 'Not *Corsica*?' as though you'd rather expected the Isle of Wight; and then it'll be all over. Hallo!"

We had just passed the narrow archway leading into the courtyard of the village and were following the path up the hill. But in that moment of passing we had been observed. Behind us a dozen village children now trailed eagerly.

"Oh, the dears!" cried Myra.

"But I think we made a mistake to bring them," I said severely. "No one is fonder of our — one, two, three . . . I make it eleven — our eleven children than I am, but there are times when Father and Mother want to be alone."

"I'm sorry, dear. I thought you'd be so proud to have them all with you."

"I *am* proud of them. To reflect that all the — one, two . . . I make it thirteen — all these thirteen are ours, is very inspiring. But I don't like people to think that we cannot afford our youngest, our little Philomene, shoes and stockings. And Giuseppe should have washed his face since last Friday. These are small matters, but they are very trying to a father."

"Have you any coppers?" asked Myra suddenly. "You forgot their pocket-money last week."

"One, two, three — I cannot possibly afford — one, two, three, four — Myra, I do wish you'd count them definitely and tell me how many we have. One likes to know. I cannot afford pocket-money for more than a dozen."

"Ten." She took a franc from me and gave it to the biggest girl. (Anne-Marie, our first, and getting on so nicely with her French.) Rapidly she explained what was to be done with it, Anne-Marie's look of intense rapture slowly straightening itself to one of ordinary gratitude as the financial standing of the other nine in the business became clear. Then we waved farewell to our family and went on.

High above the village, a thousand feet above the sea, we rested, and looked down upon the silvery olives stretching into the blue . . . and more particularly upon one red roof which stood up amid the grey-green trees.

"That's the Cardews' villa," I said.

Myra was silent.

When Myra married me she promised to love, honour and write all my thank-you-very-much letters for me, for we agreed before the ceremony that the word "obey" should mean nothing more than that. There are two sorts of T.Y.V.M. letters — the "Thank you very much for asking us, we shall be delighted to come," and the "Thank you very much for having us, we enjoyed it immensely." With these off my mind I could really concentrate on my work, or my short mashie shots, or whatever was of importance. But there was now a new kind of letter to write, and one rather outside the terms of our original understanding. A friend of mine had told his friends the Cardews that we were going out to the Riviera and would let them know when we arrived . . . and we had arrived a week ago.

"It isn't at all an easy letter to write," said Myra. "It's practically asking a stranger for hospitality."

"Let us say 'indicating our readiness to accept it.' It sounds better."

Myra smiled slowly to herself.

" 'Dear Mrs. Cardew,' " she said, " 'we are ready for lunch when you are. Yours sincerely.' "

"Well, that's the idea."

"And then what about the others? If the Cardews are going to be nice we don't want to leave Dahlia and all of them out of it."

I thought it over carefully for a little.

"What you want to do," I said at last, "is to write a really long letter to Mrs. Cardew, acquainting her with all the facts. Keep nothing back from her. I should begin by dwelling on the personnel of our little company. 'My husband and I,' you should say, 'are not alone. We have also with us Mr. and Mrs. Archibald Mannering, a delightful couple. Mr. A. Mannering is something in the Territorials when he is not looking after his estate. His wife is a great favourite in the county. Next I have to introduce to you Mr. Thomas Todd, an agreeable young bachelor. Mr. Thomas Todd

24

is in the Sucking-a-ruler-and-looking-out-of-the-window Department of the Admiralty, by whose exertions, so long as we preserve the 2 Todds to 1 formula — or, excluding Canadian Todds, 16 to 10 — Britannia rules the waves. Lastly, there is Mr. Samuel Simpson. Short of sight but warm of heart, and with (on a bad pitch) a nasty break from the off, Mr. S. Simpson is a *littérateur* of some eminence but little circulation, combining on the cornet intense wind-power with no execution, and on the golf course an endless enthusiasm with only an occasional contact. This, dear Mrs. Cardew, is our little party. I say nothing of my husband.'"

"Go on," smiled Myra. "You have still to explain how we invite ourselves to lunch."

"We don't; we leave that to her. All we do is to give a list of the meals in which, in the ordinary course, we are wont to indulge, together with a few notes on our relative capacities at each. 'Perhaps,' you wind up, 'it is at luncheon time that as a party we show to the best advantage. Some day, my dear Mrs. Cardew, we must all meet at lunch. You will then see that I have exaggerated neither my husband's appetite, nor the light conversation of my brother, nor the power of apology, should any little *contretemps* occur, of Mr. Samuel Simpson. Let us, I say, meet at lunch. Let us —'" I took out my watch suddenly.

"Come on," I said, getting up and giving a hand to Myra; "we shall only just be in time for it."

V. THE GAMESTERS

"It's about time," said Simpson one evening, "that we went to the tables and — er —" (he adjusted his spectacles) — "had a little flutter."

We all looked at him in silent admiration.

"Oh, Samuel," sighed Myra, "and I promised your aunt that you shouldn't gamble while you were away."

"But, my dear Myra, it's the first thing the fellows at the club ask you when you've been to the Riviera — if you've had any luck."

"Well, you've had a lot of luck," said Archie. "Several times when you've been standing on the heights and calling attention to the beautiful view below, I've said to myself, 'One push, and he's a deader,' but something, some mysterious agency within, has kept me back."

"All the fellows at the club —"

Simpson is popularly supposed to belong to a Fleet Street Toilet and Hairdressing Club, where for three guineas a year he gets shaved every day, and has his hair cut whenever Myra insists. On the many occasions when he authorizes a startling story of some well-known statesman with the words: "My dear old chap, I know it for a fact. I heard it at the club to-day from a friend of his," then we know that once again the barber's assistant has been gossiping over the lather.

"Do think, Samuel," I interrupted, "how much more splendid if you could be the only man who had seen Monte Carlo without going inside the rooms. And then when the hairdresser — when your friends at the club ask if you've had any luck at the tables, you just say coldly, 'What tables?' "

"Preferably in Latin," said Archie. "*Quae mensae?*"

But it was obviously no good arguing with him. Besides, we were all keen enough to go.

"We needn't lose," said Myra. "We might win."

"Good idea," said Thomas. He lit his pipe and added, "Simpson was telling me about his system last night. At least, he was just beginning when I went to sleep." He applied another match to his pipe and went on, as if the idea had suddenly struck him, "Perhaps it was only his internal system he meant. I didn't wait."

"Samuel, you *are* quite well inside, aren't you?"

"Quite, Myra. But, I *have* invented a sort of system for *roulette*, which we might —"

"There's only one system which is any good," pronounced Archie. "It's the system by which, when you've lost all your own money, you turn to the man next to you and say, 'Lend me a louis, dear old chap, till Christmas; I've forgotten my purse.' "

"No systems," said Dahlia. "Let's make a collection and put it all on one number and hope it will win."

Dahlia had obviously been reading novels about people who break the bank.

"It's as good a way of losing as any other," said Archie. "Let's do it for our first gamble, anyway. Simpson, as our host, shall put the money on. I, as his oldest friend, shall watch him to see that he does it. What's the number to be?"

We all thought hard for several moments.

"Samuel, what's your age?" asked Myra, at last.

"Right off the board," said Thomas.

"You're not really more than thirty-six?" Myra whispered to him. "Tell me as a secret."

"Peter's nearly two," said Dahlia.

"Do you think you could nearly put our money on 'two'?" asked Archie.

"I once made seventeen," I said. "On that never-to-be-forgotten day when I went in first with Archie —"

"That settles it. Here's to the highest score of The Rabbits' wicket-keeper. To-morrow afternoon we put our money on seventeen. Simpson, you have between now and 3.30 to-morrow to perfect your French delivery of the magic word *dix-sept*."

I went to bed a proud but anxious man that night. It was *my* famous score which had decided the figure that was to bring us fortune . . . and yet . . . and yet . . .

Suppose eighteen turned up? The remorse, the bitterness! "If only," I should tell myself — "if only we had run three instead of two for that cut to square-leg!" Suppose it were sixteen! "Why, oh why," I should groan, "did I make the scorer put that bye down as a hit?" Suppose it were thirty-four! But there my responsibility ended. If it were going to be thirty-four, they should have used one of Archie's scores, and made a good job of it.

At 3.30 next day we were in the fatal building. I should like to pause here and describe my costume to you, which was a quiet grey in the best of taste, but Myra says that if I do this I must describe hers too, a feat beyond me. Sufficient that she looked dazzling,

28

that as a party we were remarkably well-dressed, and that Simpson — murmuring *"dix-sept"* to himself at intervals — led the way through the rooms till he found a table to his liking.

"Aren't you excited?" whispered Myra to me.

"Frightfully," I said, and left my mouth well open. I don't quite know what picture of the event Myra and I had conjured up in our minds, but I fancy it was one something like this. At the entrance into the rooms of such a large and obviously distinguished party there would be a slight sensation among the crowd, and way would be made for us at the most important table. It would then leak out that Chevalier Simpson — the tall poetical-looking gentleman in the middle, my dear — had brought with him no less a sum than thirty francs with which to break the bank, and that he proposed to do this in one daring *coup*. At this news the players at the other tables would hastily leave their winnings (or losings) and crowd round us. Chevalier Simpson, pale but controlled, would then place his money on seventeen — *"dix-sept,"* he would say to the croupier to make it quite clear — and the ball would be spun. As it slowed down, the tension in the crowd would increase. *"Mon Dieu!"* a woman would cry in a shrill voice; there would be guttural exclamations from Germans; at the edge of the crowd strong men would swoon. At last a sudden shriek . . . and the croupier's voice, trembling for the first time for thirty years, *"Dix-sept!"* Then gold and notes would be pushed at the Chevalier. He would stuff his pockets with them; he would fill his hat with them; we others, we would stuff

29

our pockets too. The bank would send out for more money. There would be loud cheers from all the company (with the exception of one man, who had put five francs on sixteen and had shot himself) and we should be carried — that is to say, we four men — shoulder high to the door, while by the deserted table Myra and Dahlia clung to each other, weeping tears of happiness . . .

Something like that.

What happened was different. As far as I could follow, it was this. Over the heads of an enormous, badly-dressed and utterly indifferent crowd Simpson handed his thirty francs to the croupier.

"*Dix-sept*," he said.

The croupier with his rake pushed the money on to seventeen.

Another croupier with his rake pulled it off again . . . and stuck to it.

The day's fun was over.

"What *did* win?" asked Myra some minutes later, when the fact that we should never see our money again had been brought home to her.

"Zero," said Archie.

I sighed heavily.

"My usual score," I said, "not my highest."

VI. THE RECORD OF IT

"I shall be glad to see Peter again," said Dahlia, as she folded up her letter from home.

Peter's previous letter, dictated to his nurse-secretary, had, according to Archie, been full of good things. Cross-examination of the proud father, however, had failed to reveal anything more stirring than "I love mummy," and — er — so on.

We were sitting in the loggia after what I don't call breakfast — all of us except Simpson, who was busy with a mysterious package. We had not many days left; and I was beginning to feel that, personally, I should not be sorry to see things like porridge again. Each to his taste.

"The time has passed absurdly quickly," said Myra. "We don't seem to have done *anything* — except enjoy ourselves. I mean anything specially Rivierish. But it's been heavenly."

"We've done lots of Rivierish things," I protested. "If you'll be quiet a moment I'll tell you some."

These were some of the things:

(1) We had been to the Riviera. (Nothing could take away from that. We had the labels on our luggage.)

(2) We had lost heavily (thirty francs) at the Tables. (This alone justified the journey.)

(3) Myra had sat next to a Prince at lunch. (Of course she might have done this in London, but so far there has been no great rush of Princes to our little flat.

Dukes, Mayors, Companions of St. Michael and St. George, certainly; but, somehow, not Princes.)

(4) Simpson had done the short third hole at Mt. Agel in three. (His first had cleverly dislodged the ball from the piled-up tee; his second, a sudden nick, had set it rolling down the hill to the green; and the third, an accidental putt, had sunk it.)

(5) Myra and I had seen Corsica. (Question.)

(6) And finally, and best of all, we had sat in the sun, under a blue sky above a blue sea, and watched the oranges and lemons grow.

So, though we had been to but few of the famous beauty spots around, we had had a delightfully lazy time; and as proof that we had not really been at Brighton there were, as I have said, the luggage labels. But we were to be able to show further proof. At this moment Simpson came out of the house, his face beaming with excitement, his hands carefully concealing something behind his back.

"Guess what I've got," he said eagerly.

"The sack," said Thomas.

"Your new bests," said Archie.

"Something that will interest us all," helped Simpson.

"I withdraw my suggestion," said Archie.

"Something we ought to have brought with us all along."

"More money," said Myra.

The tension was extreme. It was obvious that our consuming anxiety would have to be relieved very speedily. To avoid a riot, Thomas went behind Simpson's back and took his surprise away from him.

"A camera," he said. "Good idea."

Simpson was all over himself with bon-hommy.

"I suddenly thought of it the other night," he said, smiling round at all of us in his happiness, "and I was just going to wake Thomas up to tell him, when I thought I'd keep it a secret. So I wrote to a friend of mine and asked him to send me out one, and some films and things, just as a surprise for you."

"Samuel, you *are* a dear," said Myra, looking at him lovingly.

"You see, I thought, Myra, you'd like to have some records of the place, because they're so jolly to look back on, and — er, I'm not quite sure how you work it, but I expect some of you know and — er —"

"Come on," said Myra, "I'll show you." She retired with Simpson to a secluded part of the loggia and helped him put the films in.

"Nothing can save us," said Archie. "We are going to be taken together in a group. Simpson will send it to one of the picture papers, and we shall appear as 'Another Merry Little Party of Well-known Sun-seekers. Names from left to right: Blank, blank, Mr. Archibald Mannering, blank, blank.' I'd better go and brush my hair."

Simpson returned to us, nervous and fully charged with advice.

"Right, Myra, I see. That'll be all right. Oh, look here, do you — oh yes, I see. Right. Now then — wait a bit — oh yes, I've got it. Now then, what shall we have first? A group?"

"Take the house and the garden and the village," said Thomas. "You'll see plenty of *us* afterwards."

"The first one is bound to be a failure," I pointed out. "Rather let him fail at us, who are known to be beautiful, than at the garden, which has its reputation yet to make. Afterwards, when he has got the knack, he will be able to do justice to the scenery."

Archie joined us again, followed by the bull-dog. We grouped ourselves picturesquely.

"That looks ripping," said Simpson. "Oh, look here, Myra, do you — No, don't come; you'll spoil the picture. I suppose you have to — oh, it's all right, I think I've got it."

"I shan't try to look handsome this time," said Archie; "it's not worth it. I shall just put an ordinary blurred expression on."

"Now, are you ready? Don't move. Quite still, please; quite —"

"It's instantaneous, you know," said Myra gently.

This so unnerved Simpson that he let the thing off without any further warning, before we had time to get our expressions natural.

"That was all right, Myra, wasn't it?" he said proudly.

"I'm — I'm afraid you had your hand over the lens, Samuel dear."

"Our new photographic series: 'Palms of the Great.' No. 1, Mr. S. Simpson's," murmured Archie.

"It wouldn't have been a very good one anyhow," I said encouragingly. "It wasn't typical. Dahlia should have had an orange in her hand, and Myra might have been resting her cheek against a cactus. Try it again, Simpson, and get a little more colour into it."

He tried again and got a lot more colour into it.

"Strictly speaking," said Myra sadly, "you ought to have got it on to a new film."

Simpson looked in horror at the back of his camera, found that he had forgotten to turn the handle, apologized profusely, and wound up very gingerly till the number "2" approached. "Now then," he said, looking up . . . and found himself alone.

As I write this in London I have Simpson's album in front of me. Should you ever do us the honour of dining with us (as I hope you will), and (which seems impossible) should there ever come a moment when the conversation runs low, and you are revolving in your mind whether it is worth while asking us if we have been to any theatres lately, then I shall produce the album, and you will be left in no doubt that we are just back from the Riviera. You will see oranges and lemons and olives and cactuses and palms; blue sky (if you have enough imagination) and still bluer sea; picturesque villas, curious effects of rocks, distant backgrounds of mountain . . . and on the last page the clever kindly face of Simpson.

The whole affair will probably bore you to tears.

But with Myra and me the case of course is different. We find these things, as Simpson said, very jolly to look back on.

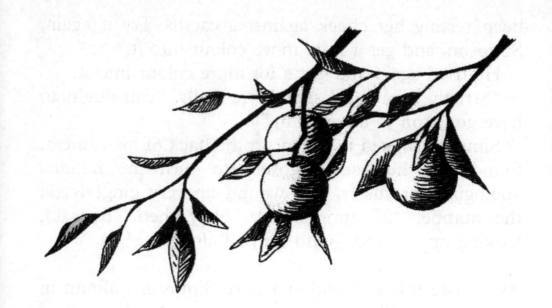

Men of Letters

John Penquarto
A Tale of Literary Life in London

(Modelled on the hundred best Authors.)

I.

John Penquarto looked round his diminutive bed-sitting-room with a feeling of excitement not unmixed with awe. So this was London! The new life had begun. With a beating heart he unpacked his bag and set out his simple belongings.

First his books, his treasured books; where should he put them? It was comforting to think that, wherever they stood, they would be within reach of his hand as he lay in bed. He placed them on the window-sill and read their titles again reverently: "Half-Hours with our Water-Beetles," "The Fretworker's Companion" and "Strenuous Days in Simla." He owed everything to them. And what an air they gave the room!

But not such an air as was given by his other treasure — the photograph of Mary.

Mary! He had only met her once, and that was twenty years ago, at his native Polwollop. He had gone to the big house with a message for Mr. Trevena, her ladyship's butler: "Mother's respects, and she has found the other shirt-front and will send it up as soon as it is dry." He had often taken a similar message, for Mrs. Penquarto did the washing for the upper servants at the Hall, but somehow he had known that to-day was going to be different.

There, just inside the gates, was Mary. He was only six, but even then he knew that never would he see again anything so beautiful. She was five; but there was something in her manner of holding herself and the imperious tilt of her head which made her seem almost five-and-a-half.

"I'm Mary," she said.

He wanted to say that he was John, but could not. He stood there tongue-tied.

"I love you," she went on.

His heart beat tumultuously. He felt suffocated. He longed to say, "So do I," but was afraid that it was not good English. Even then he knew that he must be a writer when he grew up.

She leant forward and kissed him. He realized suddenly that he was in love. The need for self-expression was strong upon him. Shyly he brought out his last acid-drop and shared it with her. He had never seen her since, but even now, twenty years after, he could not eat an acid-drop without emotion, and a whole bag of them brought the scene back so visibly as to be almost a pain.

Yes, he was to be a writer; there could be no doubt about that. Everybody had noticed it. The Vicar had said, "Johnny will never do any good at Polwollop, I fear"; and the farmer for whom John scared rooks had said, "Thiccy la-ad seems daft-like," and one after another of Mrs. Penquarto's friends had given similar testimony. And now here he was, at twenty-six, in the little bed-sitting-room in Bloomsbury, ready to write the great novel which should take London by storm. Polwollop seemed a hundred years away.

Feverishly he seized pen and paper and began to wonder what to write.

II.

It was near the Albert Memorial that the great inspiration came to him some weeks later. Those had been weeks of mingled hope and despair; of hope as he had fondled again his treasured books and read their titles, or gazed at the photograph of Mary; of despair as he had taken off his belt and counted out his rapidly-decreasing stock of money, or reflected that he was as far from completing his novel as ever. Sometimes in the search for an idea he had frequented the restaurants where the great Samuel Johnson himself had eaten, and sometimes he had frequented other restaurants where even the great Samuel Johnson himself had been unable to eat. Often he had gone into the British Museum and leant against a mummy-case, or taken a bus to Chelsea and pressed his forehead against the brass-plate which marked Carlyle's house, but no inspiration had come. And then suddenly, quite close to the Albert Memorial, he knew.

He would write a novel about a boy called William who had lived in Cornwall, and who came to London and wrote a novel, a novel of which "The Westminster Gazette" said: "This novel undoubtedly places the author in the front rank of living novelists." William's novel would be a realistic account of — yes, that was it — of a boy called Henry, who had lived in Cornwall, and who came to London and wrote a novel, a novel of which "The Morning Post" said: "By this novel the author has indubitably established his claim to be reckoned among the few living novelists who count." But stay! What should this novel of Henry's be about? It would be necessary to describe it. For an hour he wrestled with the problem, and then he had another inspiration. Henry's novel would be about a boy called Thomas who had lived in Cornwall and who came to London and wrote a novel about a boy called Stephen who had lived in Cornwall, and who came to London and wrote a novel (about a boy called Michael who had lived in Cornwall, and who came to London and wrote a novel (about a boy called Peter, who had lived in Cornwall, and . . .) . . .

And so on.

And every one of the novels would establish the author's right to be reckoned, etc., and place him undoubtedly in the very front rank.

It was a stupendous idea. For a moment John was almost paralysed at contemplation of it. There seemed to be no end to his novel as he had planned it. Was it too much for his powers?

There was only one way to find out. He hurried back to his bed-sitting-room, seized a pen and began to write.

III.

It was two years later. For the last fortnight John Penquarto had stopped counting the money in his belt. There was none left. For a fortnight now he had been living on the belt itself.

But a great hope had always sustained him. One day he would hear from the publisher to whom he had sent his novel a year ago.

And now at last the letter had come, and he was seated in the office of the great Mr. Pump himself. His heart beat rapidly. He felt suffocated.

"Well, Mr. Penquarto," said the smiling publisher, "I may say at once that we like your novel. We should have written before, but we have only just finished reading it. It is a little long — about two million eight hundred thousand words, I reckon it — but I have a suggestion to make which will meet that difficulty. I suggest that we publish it in half a dozen volumes, stopping, for the first volume, at the Press notices of (say) Peter's novel. We find that the public likes these continuous books. About terms. We will send an agreement along tomorrow. Naturally, as this is a first book, we can only pay a nominal sum on account of royalties. Say ten thousand pounds. How will that suit you?"

With a heart still beating John left the office five minutes later and bought a new belt. Then he went to a restaurant where Goldsmith had never been and ordered a joint and two veg. Success had come.

IV.

I should like to dwell upon the weeks which followed. I should like to tell of John's emotion when he saw his first proofs and of the printer's emotion when he saw what a mess John had made of them. I should like to describe how my hero's heart beat during the anxious days of waiting; to picture to you his pride at the arrival of his six free copies, and his landlady's surprise when he presented her with one. Above all, I should like to bring home to you the eagerness with which he bought and opened "The Times Literary Supplement" and read his first review:

"'William Trewulliam — The First Phase.' By John Penquarto, 7-1/2 by 5-1/4, 896 pp., Albert Pump. 9s. n."

I have no time to go into these matters, nor have I time in which to give at length his later Press cuttings, in which there was displayed a unanimity of opinion that John Penquarto was now in the front rank of living novelists, one of the limited number whose work really counted. I must hurry on.

It was a week after the publication of "William Trewulliam," the novel which had taken all London by storm. In all the drawing-rooms of Mayfair, in all the clubs of Pall Mall, people were asking each other, "Who is John Penquarto?" Nobody knew — save one.

Lady Mary knew. It was not the name Penquarto which had told her; it was — yes, you have guessed — the scene at the beginning of the book, when William Trewulliam meets the little Anne and shares his last raspberry-drop with her. Even under this disguise she recognized that early meeting. She pierced beneath the imagination of the novelist to the recollection of the man. John Penquarto — of course! Now she remembered the name.

It had always been a mystery to her friends why Lady Mary had never married. No girl in Society had been more eagerly courted. It was whispered that already she had refused more than one Archbishop, three Newspaper Proprietors and a couple of Dukes. Something, she scarcely knew what, told her that this was not love. She must wait. As she dressed to go to the Duchess of Bilberry's "At Home," she wondered if she would ever meet John Penquarto again, and if he had altered.

"Mary!"

It was John speaking. He had seen her the moment she came in at the door. Something — was it the Duchess's champagne at dinner? — had reminded him of the acid-drop they had eaten together and this had brought back his memories in a flood. To-night he would meet her again. He knew it instinctively. Besides, it was like this that William Trewulliam had met Anne again, and Henry Polhenery had met Sarah, and

Thomas Pentummas had met Alice, and — well, anyhow he knew.

"John!"

It was Mary speaking. Perhaps you had guessed.

"You knew me?" (This is John. It was his turn.)

"I knew you." (Said Mary.)

"Do you remember —"

Mary blushed, and John did not deviate from the healthy red colour which he had maintained throughout the conversation. In spite of his success he was never quite at ease in society at this period of his life. Nor were Henry Polhenery and Thomas Pentummas. They remained handsome but awkward, which was why women loved them so.

"I love you," (John speaking.)

"I think I must have always loved you." (Mary going it.)

He took her hand in his.

Nobody noticed them. They were as much alone as if they had been at the National Gallery together. Many of the guests were going through similar scenes of recognition and love-making; others were asking each other if they had read "William Trewulliam" yet, and lying about it others again were making for the buffet. John and Mary had the world to themselves . . .

V.

They were married a month later. John, who did not look his best in a frock-coat, had pleaded for a quiet

46

wedding, and only the Duchess of Bilberry and Mr. Pump were present at the simple ceremony which took place at the Bloomsbury registry-office. Then the happy couple drove away.

And where are they spending the honeymoon?

Ah, do you need to ask?

"At Greenwich?" No, fathead, not at Greenwich.

"At Clacton-on-Sea?" Look here, I don't believe you're trying. Have another shot . . .

Yes, dear reader, you are right. They are going back to Polwollop.

It might be a good plan to leave them there.

The Complete Dramatist

I take it that every able-bodied man and woman in this country wants to write a play. Since the news first got about that Orlando What's-his-name made £50,000 out of "The Crimson Sponge," there has been a feeling that only through the medium of the stage can literary art find its true expression. The successful playwright is indeed a man to be envied. Leaving aside for the moment the question of super-tax, the prizes which fall to his lot are worth something of an effort. He sees his name (correctly spelt) on buses which go to such different spots as Hammersmith and West Norwood, and his name (spelt incorrectly) beneath the photograph of somebody else in "The Illustrated Butler." He is a welcome figure at the garden-parties of the elect, who are always ready to encourage him by accepting free seats for his play; actor-managers nod to him; editors allow him to contribute without charge to a symposium on the price of golf balls. In short he becomes a "prominent figure in London Society" — and, if he is not careful, somebody will say so.

But even the unsuccessful dramatist has his moments. I knew a young man who married somebody else's mother, and was allowed by her fourteen gardeners to amuse himself sometimes by rolling the tennis-court. It was an unsatisfying life; and when rash acquaintances asked him what he did, he used to say that he was for the Bar. Now he says he is writing a play — and we look round the spacious lawns and terraces and marvel at the run his last one must have had.

However, I assume that you who read this are actually in need of the dibs. Your play must be not merely a good play, but a successful one. How shall this success be achieved?

Frankly I cannot always say. If you came to me and said, "I am on the Stock Exchange, and bulls are going down," or up, or sideways, or whatever it might be; "there's no money to be made in the City nowadays, and I want to write a play instead. How shall I do it?" — well, I couldn't help you. But suppose you said, "I'm fond of writing; my people always say my letters home are good enough for 'Punch.' I've got a little idea for a play about a man and a woman and another woman, and — but perhaps I'd better keep the plot a secret for the moment. Anyhow it's jolly exciting, and I can do the dialogue all right. The only thing is, I don't know anything about technique and stagecraft and the three unities and that sort of rot. Can you give me a few hints?" — suppose you spoke to me like this, then I could do something for you. "My dear Sir," I should reply (or Madam), "you have come to the right shop. Lend me your ear for ten minutes, and you shall learn just what stagecraft is." And I should begin with a short homily on

SOLILOQUY

If you ever read your "Shakespeare" — and no dramatist should despise the works of another dramatist; he may always pick up something in them which may be useful for his next play — if you ever read your "Shakespeare," it is possible that you have come across this passage:

"*Enter* Hamlet.

Ham. To be, or not to be —"

And, so on in the same vein for some thirty lines.

These few remarks are called a soliloquy, being addressed rather to the world in general than to any particular person on the stage. Now the object of this soliloquy is plain. The dramatist wished us to know the thoughts which were passing through Hamlet's mind, and it was the only way he could think of in which to do it. Of course, a really good actor can often give a clue to the feelings of a character simply by facial expression. There are ways of shifting the eyebrows, distending the nostrils, and exploring the lower molars with the tongue by which it is possible to denote respectively Surprise, Defiance and Doubt. Indeed, irresolution being the keynote of Hamlet's soliloquy, a clever player could to some extent indicate the whole thirty lines by a silent working of the jaw. But at the same time it would be idle to deny that he would miss the finer shades of the dramatist's meaning. "The insolence of office, and the spurns" — to take only one line — would tax the most elastic face.

So the soliloquy came into being. We moderns, however, see the absurdity of it. In real life no one thinks aloud or in an empty room. The up-to-date dramatist must certainly avoid this hallmark of the old-fashioned play.

What, then, is to be done? If it be granted, first, that the thoughts of a certain character should be known to the audience, and, secondly, that soliloquy, or the habit of thinking aloud, is in opposition to modern stage technique, how shall a soliloquy be avoided without damage to the play?

Well, there are more ways than one; and now we come to what is meant by stagecraft. Stagecraft is the art of getting over these and other difficulties, and (if possible) getting over them in a showy manner, so that people will say, "How remarkable his stagecraft is for so young a writer," when otherwise they mightn't have noticed it at all. Thus, in this play we have been talking about, an easy way of avoiding Hamlet's soliloquy would be for Ophelia to speak first.

Oph. What are you thinking about, my lord?

Ham. I am wondering whether to be or not to be, whether 'tis nobler in the mind to suffer —

And so on, till you get to the end, when Ophelia might say, "Ah, yes," or something non-committal of that sort. This would be an easy way of doing it, but it would not be the best way, for the reason that it is too easy to call attention to itself. What you want is to make it clear that you are conveying Hamlet's thoughts to the audience in rather a clever manner.

That this can now be done we have to thank the well-known inventor of the telephone. (I forget his name.) The telephone has revolutionized the stage; with its aid you can convey anything you like across the footlights. In the old badly-made play it was frequently necessary for one of the characters to take the audience into his confidence. "Having disposed of my uncle's body," he would say to the stout lady in the third row of the stalls, "I now have leisure in which to search for the will. But first to lock the door lest I should be interrupted by Harold Wotnott." In the modern well-constructed play he simply rings up an imaginary confederate and tells him what he is going to do. Could anything be more natural?

Let us, to give an example of how this method works, go back again to the play we have been discussing.

Enter Hamlet. *He walks quickly across the room to the telephone, and takes up the receiver impatiently.*

Ham. Hallo! Hallo! I want double-nine — hal-*lo*! I want double-nine two — hal-*lo*! Double-nine two three, Elsinore . . . Double-*nine*, yes . . . Hallo, is that you, Horatio? Hamlet speaking. I say, I've been wondering about this business. To be or not to be, that is the question; whether 'tis nobler in the mind to suffer the slings and arrows — What? No, Hamlet speaking. *What?* Aren't you Horatio? I want double-nine two three — sorry . . . Is that you, Exchange? You gave me double-*five*, I want double-*nine* . . . Hallo, is that you, Horatio? Hamlet speaking. I've been wondering about this business. To be or not to be, that is the — What?

No, I said, To *be* or *not* to be . . . No, "be" — b-e. Yes, that's right. To be or not to be, that is the question; whether 'tis nobler —

And so on. You see how effective it is.

But there is still another way of avoiding the soliloquy, which is sometimes used with good results. It is to let Hamlet, if that happen to be the name of your character, enter with a small dog, pet falcon, mongoose, tame bear or whatever animal is most in keeping with the part, and confide in this animal such sorrows, hopes or secret history as the audience has got to know. This has the additional advantage of putting the audience immediately in sympathy with your hero. "How *sweet* of him," all the ladies say, "to tell his little bantam about it!"

If you are not yet tired (as I am) of the Prince of Denmark, I will explain (for the last time) how a modern author might re-write his speech.

Enter Hamlet with his favourite boar-hound.

Ham. (to B.-H.). To be or not to be — ah, Fido, Fido! That is the question — eh, old Fido, boy? Whether 'tis nobler in — how now, a rat! Rats, Fido, *fetch* 'em — in the mind to suffer the slings and — *down*, Sir! — arrows — put it down! Arrows of — *drop* it, Fido; good old dog —

And so on. Which strikes me as rather sweet and natural.

Let us now pass on to the very important question of

EXITS AND ENTRANCES

To the young playwright, the difficulty of getting his characters on to the stage would seem much less than the difficulty of finding them something to say when they are there. He writes gaily and without hesitation "*Enter* Lord Arthur Fluffinose," and only then begins to bite the end of his penholder and gaze round his library for inspiration. Yet it is on that one word "Enter" that his reputation for dramatic technique will hang. Why did Lord Arthur Fluffinose enter? The obvious answer, that the firm which is mentioned in the programme as supplying his trousers would be annoyed if he didn't, is not enough; nor is it enough to say that the whole plot of the piece hinges on him, and that without him the drama would languish. What the critic wants to know is why Lord Arthur chose that very moment to come in — the very moment when Lady Larkspur was left alone in the oak-beamed hall of Larkspur Towers. Was it only a coincidence? And if the young dramatist answers callously, "Yes," it simply shows that he has no feeling for the stage whatever. In that case I needn't go on with this article.

However, it will be more convenient to assume, dear reader, that in your play Lord Arthur had a good reason for coming in. If that be so, he must explain it. It won't do to write like this: —

Enter Lord Arthur. Lady Larkspur *starts suddenly and turns towards him.*

Lady Larkspur. Arthur! You here? (*He gives a nod of confirmation. She pauses a moment, and then with a sudden passionate movement flings herself into his arms.*) Take me away, Arthur. I can't bear this life any longer. Larkspur bit me again this morning for the *third* time. I want to get away from it all. [*Swoons.*]

The subsequent scene may be so pathetic that on the hundredth night it is still bringing tears to the eyes of the fireman, but you must not expect to be treated as a serious dramatist. You will see this for yourself if you consider the passage as it should properly have been written: —

Enter Lord Arthur Fluffinose. Lady Larkspur looks at him with amazement.

Lady Larkspur. Arthur, what are you doing here?

Lord Arthur. I caught the 2.3 from town. It gets in at 3.37, and I walked over from the station. It's only a mile. (*At this point he looks at the grandfather clock in the corner, and the audience, following his eyes, sees that it is seven minutes to four, which appears delightfully natural.*) I came to tell Larkspur to sell Bungoes. They are going down.

Lady Larkspur (folding her hands over her chest and gazing broodingly at the footlights). Larkspur!

Lord Arthur (anxiously). What is it? (*Suddenly.*) Has he been ill-treating you again?

Lady Larkspur (flinging herself into his arms). Oh, Arthur, Arthur, take me away!

And so on.

But it may well be that Lord Larkspur has an intrigue of his own with his secretary, Miss Devereux, and, if their big scene is to take place on the stage too, the hall has got to be cleared for them in some way.

Your natural instinct will be to say, "*Exeunt* Fluffinose *and* Lady Larkspur, *R. Enter* Lord Larkspur *and* Miss Devereux, *L.*" This is very immature, even if you are quite clear as to which side of the stage is L. and which is R. You *must* make the evolutions seem natural. Thus: —

Enter from the left Miss Devereux. *She stops in surprise at seeing* Lord Arthur *and holds out her hand.*

Miss D. Why, Lord Arthur! Whatever —

Lord A. How d'you do? I've just run down to tell Lord Larkspur to —

Miss D. He's in the library. At least he —

Lord A. (*taking out his watch.*) Ah, then perhaps I'd better —

[Exit by door on left.]

Miss D. (*to* Lady L.). Have you seen "The Times" about here? There is a set of verses in the Financial Supplement which Lord Larkspur wanted to — (*She wanders vaguely round the room. Enter* Lord Larkspur *by door at back.*) Why, here you are! I've just sent Lord Arthur into the library to —

Lord L. I went out to speak to the gardener about —

Lady L. Ah, then I'll go and tell Arthur — *[Exit to library, leaving* Miss Devereux *and* Lord Larkspur *alone.]*

And there you are. You will, of course, appreciate that the unfinished sentences not only save time, but also make the manoeuvring very much more natural.

So far I have been writing as if you were already in the thick of your play; but it may well be that the enormous difficulty of getting the first character on has been too much for you. How, you may be wondering, are you to begin your masterpiece?

The answer to this will depend upon the length of the play, for upon the length depends the hour at which the curtain rises. If yours is an 8.15 play you may be sure that the stalls will not fill up till 8.30, and you should therefore let loose the lesser-paid members of the cast on the opening scene, keeping your fifty-pounders in reserve. In an 8.45 play the audience may be plunged into the drama at once. But this is much the more difficult thing to do, and for the beginner I should certainly recommend the 8.15 play, for which the recipe is simple.

As soon as the lights go down, and while the bald, stout gentleman is kicking our top-hat out of his way, treading heavily on our toes and wheezing, "Sorry, sorry," as he struggles to his seat, a buzz begins behind the curtain. What the players are saying is not distinguishable, but a merry girlish laugh rings out now and then, followed by the short sardonic chuckle of an obvious man of the world. Then the curtain rises, and it is apparent that we are assisting at an At Home of considerable splendour. Most of the characters seem to be on the stage, and for once we do not ask how they got there. We presume they have all been invited. Thus you have had no difficulty with your entrances.

As the chatter dies down a chord is struck on the piano.

The Bishop of Sploshington. Charming. Quite one of my favourites. Do play it again. *(Relapses into silence for the rest of the evening.)*

The Duchess of Southbridge (to Lord Reggie). Oh, Reggie, what *did* you say?

Lord Reggie (putting up his eyeglass). Said I'd bally well — top-hole — what? — don'cherknow.

Lady Evangeline (to Lady Violet, as they walk across the stage). Oh, I *must* tell you what that funny Mr. Danby said. *(Doesn't. Lady Violet, none the less, trills with happy laughter.)*

Prince von Ichdien, the well-known Ambassador (loudly, to an unnamed gentleman). What your country ought to do — *(He finishes his remarks in the lip-language, which the unnamed gentleman seems to understand. At any rate he nods several times.)*

There is more girlish laughter, more buzz and more deaf-and-dumb language. Then

Lord Tuppeny. Well, what about auction?

Amid murmurs of "You'll play, Field-Marshal?" and "Auction, Archbishop?" the crowd drifts off, leaving the hero and heroine alone in the middle of the stage.

And then you can begin.

But now I must give you a warning. You will never be a dramatist until you have learnt the technique of

MEALS

In spite of all you can do in the way of avoiding soliloquies and getting your characters on and off the stage in a dramatic manner, a time will come when you realize sadly that your play is not a bit like life after all. Then is the time to introduce a meal on the stage. A stage meal is popular, because it proves to the audience that the actors, even when called Charles Hawtrey or Owen Nares, are real people just like you and me. "Look at Mr. Bourchier eating," we say excitedly to each other in the pit, having had a vague idea up till then that an actor lived like a god on praise and greasepaint and his photograph in the papers. "Another cup, won't you?" says Miss Gladys Cooper; "No, thank you," says Mr. Dennis Eadie — dash it, it's exactly what we do at home ourselves. And when, to clinch matters, the dramatist makes Mr. Gerald du Maurier light a real cigarette in the Third Act, then he can flatter himself that he has indeed achieved the ambition of every stage writer, and "brought the actual scent of the hay across the footlights."

But there is a technique to be acquired in this matter as in everything else within the theatre. The great art of the stage-craftsman, as I have already shown, is to seem natural rather than to be natural. Let your actors have tea by all means, but see that it is a properly histrionic tea. This is how it should go: —

Hostess. How do you do? You'll have some tea, won't you? *[Rings bell.]*

Guest. Thank you.

Enter Butler.

Hostess. Tea, please, Matthews.

Butler (impassively). Yes, m'lady. *(This is all he says during the play, so he must try and get a little character into it, in order that "The Era" may remark, "Mr. Thompson was excellent as Matthews." However, his part is not over yet, for he returns immediately,* followed by three footmen — *just as it happened when you last called on the Duchess* — *and sets out the tea.*)

Hostess (holding up the property lump of sugar in the tongs). Sugar?

Guest (luckily). No, thanks.

Hostess replaces lump and inclines empty teapot over tray for a moment; then hands him a cup painted brown inside — thus deceiving the gentleman with the telescope in the upper circle.

Guest (touching his lips with the cup and then returning it to its saucer). Well, I must be going.

Re-enter Butler and three Footmen, who remove the tea-things.

Hostess (to Guest). Good-bye; so glad you could come. [*Exit* Guest.]

His visit has been short, but it has been very thrilling while it lasted.

Tea is the most usual meal on the stage, for the reason that it is the least expensive, the property lump of sugar being dusted and used again on the next night. For a stage dinner a certain amount of genuine sponge-cake has to be made up to look like fish, chicken or cutlet. In novels the hero has often "pushed his meals away untasted," but no stage hero would do anything so unnatural as this. The etiquette is to have two bites before the butler and the three footmen whisk away the plate. Two bites are made, and the bread is crumbled, with an air of great eagerness; indeed, one feels that in real life the guest would clutch hold of the footman and say, "Half a mo', old chap, I haven't *nearly* finished"; but the actor is better schooled than

60

this. Besides, the thing is coming back again as chicken directly.

But it is the cigarette which chiefly has brought the modern drama to its present state of perfection. Without the stage cigarette many an epigram would pass unnoticed, many an actor's hands would be much more noticeable; and the man who works the fireproof safety curtain would lose even the small amount of excitement which at present attaches to his job.

Now although it is possible, in the case of a few men at the top of the profession, to leave the conduct of the cigarette entirely to the actor, you will find it much more satisfactory to insert in the stage directions the particular movements (with match and so forth) that you wish carried out. Let us assume that Lord Arthur asks Lord John what a cynic is — the question of what a cynic is having arisen quite naturally in the course of the plot. Let us assume further that you wish Lord John to reply, "A cynic is a man who knows the price of everything and the value of nothing." It has been said before, but you may feel that it is quite time it was said again; besides, for all the audience knows, Lord John may simply be quoting. Now this answer, even if it comes quite fresh to the stalls, will lose much of its effect if it is said without the assistance of a cigarette. Try it for yourself.

Lord John. A cynic is a man who, etc . . .

Rotten. Now try again.

Lord John. A cynic is a man who, etc . . . *[Lights cigarette.]*

No, even that is not good. Once more: —

Lord John (lighting cigarette). A cynic is a man who, etc.

Better, but leaves too much to the actor.

Well, I see I must tell you.

Lord John (taking out gold cigarette case from his left-hand upper waistcoat pocket). A cynic, my dear Arthur *(he opens case deliberately, puts cigarette in mouth, and extracts gold match-box from right-hand trouser)* is a man who *(strikes match)* knows the price of *(lights cigarette)* — everything, and *(standing with match in one hand and cigarette in the other)* the value of — pff *(blows out match)* of — nothing.

It makes a different thing of it altogether. Of course on the actual night the match may refuse to strike, and Lord John may have to go on saying "a man who — a man who — a man who" until the ignition occurs, but even so it will still seem delightfully natural to the audience (as if he were making up the epigram as he went along); while as for blowing the match out, he can hardly fail to do *that* in one.

The cigarette, of course, will be smoked at other moments than epigrammatic ones, but on these other occasions you will not need to deal so fully with it in the stage directions. "*Duke (lighting cigarette).* I trust, Perkins, that . . ." is enough. You do not want to say, "*Duke (dropping ash on trousers).* It seems to me, my love . . ." or, "*Duke (removing stray piece of tobacco from tongue).* What Ireland needs is . . ."; still less "*Duke (throwing away end of cigarette).* Show him in." For this must remain one of the mysteries of the stage — What happens to the stage cigarette when it has been

62

puffed four times? The stage tea, of which a second cup is always refused; the stage cutlet, which is removed with the connivance of the guest after two mouthfuls; the stage cigarette, which nobody ever seems to want to smoke to the end — thinking of these as they make their appearances in the houses of the titled, one would say that the hospitality of the peerage was not a thing to make any great rush for . . .

But that would be to forget the butler and the three footmen. Even a Duke cannot have everything. And what his *chef* may lack in skill his butler more than makes up for in impassivity.

A Poetry Recital

It has always been the privilege of Art to be patronized by Wealth and Rank. Indeed, if we literary and artistic strugglers were not asked out to afternoon tea sometimes by our millionaire acquaintances, it is doubtful if we should be able to continue the struggle. Recently a new (and less expensive) method of entertaining Genius has become fashionable in the best circles, and the aspiring poet is now invited to the house of the Great, not for the purpose of partaking of bodily refreshment himself, but in order that he may afford spiritual refreshment to others. In short, he is given an opportunity of reciting his own works in front of the Fair, the Rich and the Highly Born, and making what he can out of it in the way of advertisement.

Let us imagine that we have been lucky enough to secure an invitation to one of Lady Poldoodle's Poetry At-Homes, at her charming little house in Berkeley Square.

The guests are all waiting, their eyes fixed in eager anticipation on the black-covered throne at the farther end of the room, whereon each poet will sit to declaim his masterpiece, when suddenly Lord Poldoodle is observed to be making his way cautiously towards a side-door. Fortunately he is stopped in time, and dragged back to his seat next to the throne, from which he rises a moment later to open the proceeding.

"Ladies and gentlemen," he says, "we are met here this afternoon in order to listen to some of our younger poets who will recite from their own works. So far, I have always managed to avoid — so far, I have been unavoidably prevented from attending on these occasions, but I understand that the procedure is as follows. Each poet will recite a short sample of his poetry, after which, no doubt, you will go home and order from your bookseller a complete set of his works."

Lady Poldoodle goes quickly over to him and whispers vigorously.

"I find I am wrong," says our host. "Full sets of the author's works can be obtained on the way out. There is, however, no compulsion in the matter, and, if you take my advice — well, well, let us get on. Our first poet" — here he puts on his glasses, and reads from a paper on the table in front of him — "is Mr. Sydney Worple, of whom you — er — have — er — doubtless all heard. At any rate you will hear him now."

Mr. Sydney Worple, tall and thin, wearing the sort of tie which makes you think you must have seen him before, steps forward amidst applause. He falls back into the throne as if deep in thought, and passes a hand across his hair.

Mr. Worple (*very suddenly*) "Dawn at Surbiton."

"Where?" says a frightened voice at the back.

"H'sh!" says Lady Poldoodle in a whisper. "Surbiton."

"Surbiton" is passed round the back seats. Not that it is going to matter in the least.

Mr. Worple repeats the title, and then recites in an intense voice these lines:

> Out of the nethermost bonds of night,
>   Out of the gloom where the bats' wings brush
>   me,
>   Free from the crepitous doubts which crush
>   me,
> Forth I fare to the cool sunlight;
>
> Forth to a world where the wind sweeps clean,
>   Where the smooth-limbed ash to the blue
>   stands bare,
>   And the gossamer spreads her opalled ware —
> And Jones is catching the 8.15.

After several more verses like this he bows and retires. Lady Poldoodle, still mechanically clapping, says to her neighbour:

"How beautiful! Dawn at Surbiton! Such a beautiful idea, I think."

"Wasn't it sublime?" answers the neighbour. "The wonderful contrast between the great pageant of nature and poor Mr. Jones, catching — always catching — the 8.15."

But Lord Poldoodle is rising again. "Our next poet," he says, "is Miss Miranda Herrick, whose work is so distinguished for its — er — its — er — distinction."

Miss Herrick, dressed in pale green and wearing pincenez, flutters in girlishly. She gives a nervous little giggle, pushes out her foot, withdraws it and begins:

When I take my bath in the morning —

The audience wakes up with a start. "When you take your *what!*" says Lord Poldoodle.

Miss Herrick begins again, starting this time with the title.

LIFE

When I take my bath in the morning,
When I strip for the cool delight,
   And the housemaid brings
   Me towels and things,
Do I reck of the coming night?

A materially-minded man whispers to his neighbour that *he* always wonders what's for breakfast. "H'sh!" she says, for there is another verse to come.

When my hair comes down in the evening,
And my tired clothes swoon to the ground,
   Do I bother my head,
   As I leap in bed,
Of the truth which the dawn brings round?

In the uncomfortable pause which follows, a voice is heard saying, "Does she?" and Lady Poldoodle asks kindly, "Is that all, dear?"

"What more could there be?" says Miss Herrick with a sigh. "What more is there to say? It is Life."

"Life! How true!" says the hostess. "But won't you give us something else? That one ended so very suddenly."

After much inward (and outward) wrestling Miss Herrick announces:

A THOUGHT

The music falls across the vale
From nightingale to nightingale;
The owl within the ivied tree
Makes love to me, makes love to me;
But all the tadpoles in the pond
Are dumb — however fond.

"I begin to think that there is something in a tadpole after all," murmurs Lord Poldoodle to himself, as the author wriggles her way out.

"After all," says one guest to another, "why shouldn't a tadpole make love as much as anybody else?"

"I think," says her neighbour, "that the idea is of youth trying vainly to express itself — or am I thinking of caterpillars? Lord Poldoodle, what is a tadpole exactly?"

"A tadpole," he answers decisively, "is an extremely immature wriggling creature, which is, quite rightly, dumb."

Now steps forward Mr. Horatio Bullfinch, full of simple enthusiasm, one of the London school. He gives us his famous poem, "Berkeley Square."

The men who come from the north country
    Are tall and very fair,
The men who come from the south country
    Have hardly any hair,
But the only men in the world for me
    Are the men of Berkeley Square.

The sun may shine at Colchester,
    The rain may rain at Penge;
From low-hung skies the dawn may rise
    Broodingly on Stonehenge.
Knee-deep in clover the lambs at Dover
    Nibble awhile and stare;
But there's only one place in the world for me,
    Berkeley — Berkeley Square.

And so on, down to that magnificent last verse:

The skylark triumphs from the blue,
    Above the barley fields at Loo,
The blackbird whistles loud and clear
    Upon the hills at Windermere;
But oh, I simply LOVE the way
    Our organ-grinder plays all day!

Lord Poldoodle rises to introduce Mr. Montagu
Mott.

"Mr. Mott," he says, "is, I am told, our leading
exponent of what is called *vers libre*, which means —
well, you will see what it means directly."

69

Mr. Mott, a very ugly little man, who tries to give you the impression that he is being ugly on purpose, and could easily be beautiful if he were not above all that sort of thing, announces the title of his masterpiece. It is called "Why Is the Fat Woman's Face So Red?" Well, what else *could* you call it?

Why is the fat woman's face so red?
Is it because her stays are too tight?
Or because she wants to sneeze and has lost her
    pocket handkerchief?
Or only because her second son
(The engineer)
Is dying of cancer.
I cannot be certain.
Yet I sit here and ask myself
Wonderingly
Why is the fat woman's face so red?

It is generally recognized that, in Mr. Mott, we have a real poet. There are loud cries of "Encore!" Mr. Mott shakes his head.

"I have written no more," he says in a deep voice. "I have given you the result of three years' work. Perhaps — in another three years —" He shrugs his shoulders and walks gloomingly out.

"Such a sweet idea," says Lady Poldoodle. "I sit here and ask myself — wonderingly! How true! How very true!"

"I couldn't quite follow it, dear," says her neighbour frankly. "Did he marry her after all?"

Lord Poldoodle, looking slightly more cheerful, gets once more on to his legs.

"You will all be very glad to hear — ah — you will all be sorry to hear that we have only one more poet on our list this afternoon. Mr. Cecil Willow, the well-known — er — poet."

Mr. Willow, a well-dressed young man, fair and rather stout, and a credit to any drawing-room, announces the subject of his poem — Liberty.

"Liberty, what crimes have been committed in thy name!" murmurs Lord Poldoodle to himself.

LIBERTY

There were two thrushes in a tree,
The one was tamed, the other free.
Because his wings were clipped so small
The tame one did not fly at all,
But sang to Heaven all the day —
The other (shortly after) flew away.

There were two women in a town,
The one was blonde, the other brown.
The brown one pleased a Viscount's son
(Not Richard, but the other one)
He gave her a delightful flat —
The blonde one loved a man called Alfred Spratt.

There were two Kings on thrones of gold,
The one was young, the other old.
The young one's laws were wisely made

Till someone took a hand-grenade
And threw it, shouting, "Down with Kings!" —
The old one laid foundation stones and things.

"How delightful," says everybody. "How very delightful. Thank you, Lady Poldoodle, for such a delightful afternoon."

The Perils of Reviewing

A most unfortunate thing has happened to a friend of mine called — to a friend of — to a — . Well, I suppose the truth will have to come out. It happened to me. Only don't tell anybody.

I reviewed a book the other day. It is not often I do this, because before one can review a book one has to, or is supposed to, read it, which wastes a good deal of time. Even that isn't an end of the trouble. The article which follows is not really one's own, for the wretched fellow who wrote the book is always trying to push his way in with his views on matrimony, or the Sussex downs, or whatever his ridiculous subject is. He expects one to say, "Mr. Blank's treatment of Hilda's relations with her husband is masterly," whereas what one wants to say is, "Putting Mr. Blank's book on one side, we may consider the larger question, whether —" and so consider it (alone) to the end of the column.

Well, I reviewed Mr. Blank's book, "Rotundity." As I expected, the first draft had to be re-headed "A Corner of old London," and used elsewhere; Mr. Blank didn't get into it at all. I kept promising myself a sentence: "Take 'Rotundity,' for instance, the new novel by William Blank, which, etc." but before I was ready for it the article was finished. In my second draft, realizing the dangers of delay, I began at once, "This remarkable novel," and continued so for a couple of sentences. But on reading it through afterwards I saw at once that the first two sentences were out of place in an article that obviously ought to be called "The Last Swallow"; so I cut them out, sent "The Last Swallow: A Reverie" to another Editor, and began again. The third time I was successful.

Of course in my review I said all the usual things. I said that Mr. Blank's attitude to life was "subjective rather than objective" . . . and a little lower down that it was "objective rather than subjective." I pointed out that in his treatment of the major theme he was a neo-romanticist, but I suggested that, on the other hand, he had nothing to learn from the Russians — or the Russians had nothing to learn from him; I forget which. And finally I said (and this is the cause of the whole trouble) that Antoine Vaurelle's world-famous classic — and I looked it up in the encyclopedia — world-renowned classic, "Je Comprends Tout," had been not without its influence on Mr. Blank. It was a good review, and the editor was pleased about it.

A few days later Mr. Blank wrote to say that, curiously enough, he had never read "Je Comprends Tout." It didn't seem to me very curious, because I had never read it either, but I thought it rather odd of him to confess as much to a stranger. The only book of Vaurelle's which I had read was "Consolatrice," in an English translation. However, one doesn't say these things in a review.

Now I have a French friend, Henri, one of those annoying Frenchmen who talk English much better than I do, and Henri, for some extraordinary reason, had seen my review. He has to live in London now, but his heart is in Paris; and I imagine that every word of his beloved language which appears, however casually, in an English paper mysteriously catches his eye and brings the scent and sounds of the boulevards to him across the coffee-cups. So, the next time I met him, he shook me warmly by the hand, and told me how glad he was that I was an admirer of Antoine Vaurelle's novels.

"Who isn't?" I said with a shrug, and, to get the conversation on to safer ground, I added hastily that in some ways I almost liked "Consolatrice" best.

He shook my hand again. So did he. A great book.

"But of course," he said, "one must read it in the original French. It is the book of all others which loses by translation."

"Of course," I agreed. Really, I don't see what else I could have done.

"Do you remember that wonderful phrase —" and he rattled it off. "Magnificent, is it not?"

"Magnificent," I said, remembering an appointment instead. "Well, I must be getting on. Good-bye." And, as I walked off, I patted my forehead with my handkerchief and wondered why the day had grown so warm suddenly.

However the next day was even warmer. Henri came to see me with a book under his arm. We all have one special book of our own which we recommend to our acquaintances, regarding the love of it as perhaps the best passport to our friendship. This was Henri's. He was about to test me. I had read and admired his favourite Vaurelle — in the original French. Would I love his darling Laforgue? My reputation as a man, as a writer, as a critic, depended on it. He handed me the book — in French.

"It is all there," he said reverently, as he gave it to me. "All your English masters, they all come from him. Perhaps, most of all, your — But you shall tell me when you have read it. You shall tell me whom most you seem to see there. Your Meredith? Your Shaw? Your — But you shall tell me."

"I will tell you," I said faintly.

And I've got to tell him.

Don't think that I shall have any difficulty in reading the book. Glancing through it just now I came across this: —

" '*Kate, avez-vous soupé avant le spectacle?*'
'*Non, je n'avais guère le coeur à manger.*' "

Well, that's easy enough. But I doubt if it is one of the most characteristic passages. It doesn't give you a clue to Laforgue's manner, any more than " 'Must I sit here, mother?' 'Yes, without a doubt you must,' " tells you all that you want to know about Meredith. There's more in it than that.

And I've got to tell him.

But fancy holding forth on an author's style after reading him laboriously with a dictionary!

However, I must do my best; and in my more hopeful moments I see the conversation going like this: —

"Well?"

"Oh, wonderful." (*With emotion*) "Really wonderful."

"You see them all there?"

"Yes, yes. It's really — wonderful. Meredith — I mean — well, it's simply — (*after a pause*) wonderful."

"You see Meredith there most?"

"Y-yes. Sometimes. And then (*with truth*) sometimes I — I don't. It's difficult to say. Sometimes I — er — Shaw — er — well, it's —" (*with a gesture somewhat Gallic*) "How can I put it?"

"Not Thackeray at all?" he says, watching me eagerly. I decide to risk it.

"Oh, but of course! I mean — Thackeray! When I said Meredith I was thinking of the *others*. But Thackeray — I mean Thackeray *is* — er —" (*I've forgotten the author's name for the moment and go on hastily*) "I mean — er — Thackeray, obviously."

He shakes me by the hand. I am his friend.

But this conversation only takes place in my more hopeful moments. In my less hopeful ones I see myself going into the country for quite a long time.

Summer Days

The Competition Spirit

About six weeks ago a Canadian gentleman named Smith arrived in the Old Country (England). He knew a man who knew a man who knew a man . . . and so on for a bit . . . who knew a man who knew a man who knew me. Letters passed; negotiations ensued; and about a week after he had first set foot in the Mother City (London), Smith and I met at my Club for lunch.

I may confess now that I was nervous. I think I expected a man in a brown shirt and leggings, who would ask me to put it "right there," and tell me I was "some Englishman." However, he turned out to be exactly like anybody else in London. Whether he found me exactly like anybody else in Canada I don't know. Anyway, we had a very pleasant lunch, and arranged to play golf together on the next day.

Whatever else is true of Canada there can be no doubt that it turns out delightful golfers. Smith proved to be just the best golfer I had ever met, being, when at the top of his form, almost exactly as good as I was. Hole after hole we halved in a mechanical eight. If by means of a raking drive and four perfect brassies at the sixth he managed to get one up for a moment, then at the short seventh a screaming iron and three consummate approaches would make me square again. Occasionally he would, by superhuman play, do a hole in bogey; but only to crack at the next, and leave me, at the edge of the green, to play "one off eleven." It was, in fact, a ding-dong struggle all the way; and for his one-hole victory in the morning I had my revenge with a one-hole victory in the afternoon.

By the end of a month we must have played a dozen rounds of this nature. I always had a feeling that I was really a better golfer than he, and this made me friendly towards his game. I would concede him short putts which I should have had no difficulty in missing myself; if he lost his ball I would beg him to drop another and go on with the hole; if he got into a bad place in a bunker I would assure him it was ground under repair. He was just as friendly in refusing to take these advantages, just as pleasant in offering similar indulgences to me. I thought at first it was part of his sporting way, but it turned out that (absurdly enough) he also was convinced that he was really the better golfer of the two, and could afford these amenities.

One day he announced that he was going back to Canada.

"We must have a last game," he said, "and this one must be decisive."

"For the championship of the Empire," I agreed. "Let's buy a little cup and play for it. I've never won anything at golf yet, and I should love to see a little cup on the dinner-table every night."

"You can't come to dinner in Canada every night," he pointed out. "It would be so expensive for you."

Well, the cup was bought, engraved "The Empire Challenge Cup," and played for last Monday.

"This," said Smith, "is a serious game, and we must play all out. No giving away anything, no waiving the rules. The Empire is at stake. The effeteness of the Mother Country is about to be put to the proof. Proceed."

It wasn't the most pleasant of our games. The spirit of the cup hung over it and depressed us. At the third hole I had an eighteen-inch putt for a half. "That's all right," said Smith forgetfully; and then added, "Perhaps you'd better put it in, though." Of course I missed. On the fifth green he was about to brush away a leaf. "That's illegal," I said sharply, "you must pick it up; you mayn't brush it away," and after a fierce argument on the point he putted hastily — and badly. At the eighteenth tee we were all square and hardly on speaking terms. The fate of the Mother Country depended upon the result of this hole.

I drove a long one, the longest of the day, slightly hooked.

"Good shot," said Smith with an effort. He pressed and foozled badly. I tried not to look pleased.

We found his ball in a thick clump of heather. With a grim look on his face, he took out his niblick . . .

I stayed by him and helped him count up to eight.

"Where's your ball?" he growled.

"A long way on," I said reproachfully. "I wish you'd hurry up. The poor thing will be getting cold."

He got to work again. We had another count together up to fifteen. Sometimes there would be a gleam of white at the top of the heather for a moment and then it would fade away.

"How many?" I asked some minutes later.

"About thirty. But I don't care, I'm going to get the little beast into the hole if it takes me all night." He went on hacking.

I had lost interest in the performance, for the cup was mine, but I did admire his Colonial grit.

"Got it," he cried suddenly, and the ball sailed out on to the pretty. Another shot put him level with me.

"Thirty-two?" I asked.

"About," he said coldly.

I began to look for my ball. It had got tired of waiting and had hidden itself. Smith joined gloomily in the search.

"This is absurd," I said, after three or four minutes.

"By jove!" said Smith, suddenly brightening up. "If your ball's lost I win after all."

"Nonsense; you've given the hole up," I protested. "You don't know how many you've played. According to the rules, if I ask you how many, and you give wrong information —"

"It's thirty-five," he said promptly.

"I don't believe you counted."

"Call it forty-five then. There's nothing to prevent my calling it more than it really is. If it was really only forty, then I'm counting five occasions when the ball rolled over as I was addressing it. That's very generous of me. Actually I'm doubtful if the ball did roll over five times, but I say it did in order to be on the safe side."

He looked at his watch. "And if you don't find your ball in thirty seconds, you lose the hole."

It was ingenious, but the Mother Country can be ingenious too.

"How many have you played exactly?" I asked. "Be careful."

"Forty-five," he said. "Exactly."

"Right." I took my niblick and swung at the heather. "Bother," I said. "Missed it. Two."

"Hallo! Have you found it?"

"I have. It's somewhere in this field. There's no rule which insists that you shall hit the ball, or even that you shall hit near the ball, or even that you shall see the ball when you hit at it. Lots of old gentlemen shut their eyes and miss the sphere. I've missed. In five minutes I shall miss again."

"But what's the point?"

"The point, dear friend," I smiled, "is that after each stroke one is allowed five minutes in which to find the ball. I have forty-three strokes in hand; that gives me three hours and thirty-five minutes in which to look for it. At regular intervals of five minutes I shall swing my club and probably miss. It's four-thirty now; at eight o'clock, unless I find my ball before, I shall be playing the like. And if you are a sportsman," I added, "you will bring me out some tea in half an hour."

At six-thirty I was still looking — and swinging. Smith then came to terms and agreed to share the cup with me for the first year. He goes back to Canada to-morrow, and will spread the good news there that the Old Country can still hold its own in resource, determination and staying power. But next year we are going to play friendly golf again.

A Song for the Summer

Is it raining? Never mind —
Think how much the birdies love it!
See them in their dozens drawn,
Dancing, to the croquet lawn —
Could our little friends have dined
If there'd been no worms above it?

Is it murky? What of that,
If the Owls are fairly perky?
Just imagine you were one —
Wouldn't you *detest* the sun?
I'm pretending I'm a Bat,
And I know I *like* it murky.

Is it chilly? After all,
We must not forget the Poodle.
If the days were really hot,
Could he wear *one* woolly spot?
Could he even keep his shawl?
No, he'd shave the whole caboodle.

The Enchanted Castle

There are warm days in London when even a window-box fails to charm, and one longs for the more open spaces of the country. Besides, one wants to see how the other flowers are getting on. It is on these days that we travel to our Castle of Stopes; as the crow flies, fifteen miles away. Indeed, that is the way we get to it, for it is a castle in the air. And when we are come to it, Celia is always in a pink sunbonnet gathering roses lovingly, and I, not very far off, am speaking strongly to somebody or other about something I want done. By-and-by I shall go into the library and work . . . with an occasional glance through the open window at Celia.

To think that a month ago we were quite happy with a few pink geraniums! Sunday, a month ago, was hot. "Let's take the train somewhere," said Celia, "and have lunch under a hedge."

"I know a lovely place for hedges," I said.

"I know a lovely tin of potted grouse," said Celia, and she went off to cut some sandwiches. By twelve o'clock we were getting out of the train.

The first thing we came to was a golf course, and Celia had to drag me past it. Then we came to a wood, and I had to drag her through it. Another mile along a lane, and then we both stopped together.

"Oh!" we said.

It was a cottage, the cottage of a dream. And by a cottage I mean, not four plain rooms and a kitchen, but one surprising room opening into another; rooms all on different levels and of different shapes, with delightful places to bump your head on; open fireplaces; a large square hall, oak-beamed, where your guests can hang about after breakfast, while deciding whether to play golf or sit in the garden. Yet all so cunningly disposed that from outside it looks only a cottage or, at most, two cottages persuaded into one.

And, of course, we only saw it from outside. The little drive, determined to get there as soon as possible, pushed its way straight through an old barn, and arrived at the door simultaneously with the flagged lavender walk for the humble who came on foot. The rhododendrons were ablaze beneath the south windows; a little orchard was running wild on the west; there was a hint at the back of a clean-cut lawn. Also, you remember, there was a golf course, less than two miles away.

"Oh," said Celia with a deep sigh, "but we must live here."

An Irish terrier ran out to inspect us. I bent down and patted it. "With a dog," I added.

"Isn't it all lovely? I wonder who it belongs to, and if —"

"If he'd like to give it to us."

"Perhaps he would if he saw us and admired us very much," said Celia hopefully.

"I don't think Mr. Barlow is that sort of man," I said. "An excellent fellow, but not one to take these sudden fancies."

"Mr. Barlow? How do you know his name?"

"I have these surprising intuitions," I said modestly. "The way the chimneys stand up —"

"I know," cried Celia. "The dog's collar."

"Right, Watson. And the name of the house is Stopes."

She repeated it to herself with a frown.

"What a disappointing name," she said. "Just Stopes."

"Stopes," I said. "Stopes, Stopes. If you keep on saying it, a certain old-world charm seems to gather round it. Stopes."

"Stopes," said Celia. "It *is* rather jolly."

We said it ten more times each, and it seemed the only possible name for it. Stopes — of course.

"Well!" I asked.

"We must write to Mr. Barlow," said Celia decisively. " 'Dear Mr. Barlow, er — Dear Mr. Barlow — we —' Yes, it will be rather difficult. What do we want to say exactly?"

" 'Dear Mr. Barlow — May we have your house?' "

"Yes," smiled Celia, "but I'm afraid we can hardly ask for it. But we might rent it when — when he doesn't want it any more."

" 'Dear Mr. Barlow,' " I amended, " 'have you any idea when you're going to die?' No, that wouldn't do either. And there's another thing — we don't know his initials, or even if he's a 'Mr.' Perhaps he's a knight or a

— a duke. Think how offended Duke Barlow would be if we put ' — Barlow, Esq.' on the envelope."

"We could telegraph. 'Barlow. After you with Stopes.'"

"Perhaps there's a young Barlow, a Barlowette or two with expectations. It may have been in the family for years."

"Then we — Oh, let's have lunch." She sat down and began to undo the sandwiches. "Dear o' Stopes," she said with her mouth full.

We lunched outside Stopes. Surely if Earl Barlow had seen us he would have asked us in. But no doubt his dining-room looked the other way; towards the east and north, as I pointed out to Celia, thus being pleasantly cool at lunch-time.

"Ha, Barlow," I said dramatically, "a time will come when *we* shall be lunching in there, and *you* — bah!" And I tossed a potted-grouse sandwich to his dog.

However, that didn't get us any nearer.

"Will you *promise*," said Celia, "that we shall have lunch in there one day?"

"I promise," I said readily. That gave me about sixty years to do something in.

"I'm like — who was it who saw something of another man's and wouldn't be happy till he got it?"

"The baby in the soap advertisement."

"No, no, some king in history."

"I believe you are thinking of Ahab, but you aren't a bit like him, really. Besides, we're not coveting Stopes. All we want to know is, does Barlow ever let it in the summer?"

"That's it," said Celia eagerly.

"And, if so," I went on, "will he lend us the money to pay the rent with?"

"Er — yes," said Celia. "That's it."

So for a month we have lived in our Castle of Stopes. I see Celia there in her pink sun-bonnet, gathering the flowers lovingly, bringing an armful of them into the hall, disturbing me sometimes in the library with "*Aren't* they beauties? No, I only just looked in — good luck to you." And she sees me ordering a man about importantly, or waving my hand to her as I ride through the old barn on my road to the golf course.

But this morning she had an idea.

"Suppose," she said timidly, "you *wrote* about Stopes, and Mr. Barlow happened to see it, and knew how much we wanted it, and —"

"Well!"

"Then," said Celia firmly, "if he were a gentleman he would give it to us."

Very well. Now we shall see if Mr. Barlow is a gentleman.

The Sands of Pleasure

Ladies first, so we will start with Jenny. Jenny is only nine, but she has been to the seaside before and knows all about it. She wears the fashionable *costume de plage*, which consists of a white linen hat, a jersey and an overcrowded pair of bathing-drawers, into which not only Jenny, but the rest of her wardrobe, has had to fit itself. Two slim brown legs emerge to bear the burden, and one feels that if she fell over she would have to stay there until somebody picked her up.

She is holding Richard Henry by the hand. Richard Henry is four, and this is the first time he has seen the sea. Jenny is showing it to him. Privately he thinks that it has been over-rated. There was a good deal of talk about it in his suburb (particularly from Jenny, who had been there before) and naturally one expected something rather — well, rather more like what they had been saying it was like. However, perhaps it would be as well to keep in with Jenny and not to let her see that he is disappointed, so every time she says, "Isn't the sea lovely?" he echoes, "Lovely," and now and then he adds (just to humour her), "Is 'at the sea?" and then she has the chance to say again, "Yes, that's the sea, darling. Isn't it lovely?" It is obvious that she is proud of it. Apparently she put it there. Anyway, it seems to be hers now.

Jenny has brought Father and Mother as well as Richard Henry. There they are, over there. When she came before she had to leave them behind, much to their disappointment. Father was saying, "Form fours, left," before going off to France again, and Mother was buying wool to make him some more socks. It was a great relief to them to know that they were being taken this time, and that they would have Jenny to tell them all about it.

Father is lying in a deck-chair, smoking his pipe. There has been an interesting discussion this afternoon as to whether he is a coward or not. Father thought he wasn't, but Mother wasn't quite so sure. Jenny said that of course he couldn't really be, because the King gave him a medal for not being one, but Mother explained that it was only a medal he had over, and Father happened to be passing by the window.

"I don't see what this has to do with it," said Father. "I simply prefer bathing in the morning."

"Oo, you said this morning you preferred bathing in the afternoon," says Jenny like a flash.

"I know; but since then I've had time to think it over, and I see that I was hasty. The morning is the best time."

"I'm afraid he *is* a coward," said Mother sadly, wondering why she had married him.

"The whole point is, why did Jenny bring me here?"

"To enjoy yourself," said Jenny promptly.

"Well, I am," said Father, closing his eyes.

But we do not feel so sure that Mother is enjoying herself. She has just read in the paper about a mine that

95

floated ashore and exploded. Nobody was near at the time, but supposing one of the children had been playing with it.

"Which one?" said Father lazily.

"Jenny."

"Then we should have lost Jenny."

This being so, Jenny promises solemnly not to play with any mine that comes ashore, nor to let Richard Henry play with it, nor to allow it to play with Richard Henry, nor —

"I suppose I may just point it out to him and say, 'Look, that's a mine'?" says Jenny wistfully. If she can't do this, it doesn't seem to be much use coming to the seaside at all.

"I don't think there would be any harm in that," says Father. "But don't engage it in conversation."

"Thank you very much," says Jenny, and she and Richard Henry go off together.

Mother watches them anxiously. Father closes his eyes.

"Now," says Jenny eagerly, "I'm going to show you a darling little crab. Won't that be lovely?"

Richard Henry, having been deceived, as he feels, about the sea, is not too hopeful about that crab. However, he asks politely, "What's a crab?"

"You'll see directly, darling," says Jenny; and he has to be content with that.

"Crab," he murmurs to himself.

Suddenly an idea occurs to him. He lets go of Jenny's hand and trots up to an old gentleman with white whiskers.

"Going to see a crab," he announces.

"Going to see a crab, are you, my little man?" says the old gentleman kindly.

"Going to see a crab," says Richard Henry, determined to keep up his end of the conversation.

"Well, I never! So you're going to see a crab!" says the old gentleman, doing his best with it.

Richard Henry nods two or three times. "Going to see a crab," he says firmly.

Luckily Jenny comes up and rescues him, otherwise they would still be at it. "Come along, darling, and see the crab," she says, picking up his hand; and Richard Henry looks triumphantly at the old gentleman. There you are. Perhaps he will believe a fellow another time.

Jenny has evidently made an arrangement with a particular crab for this afternoon. It is to be hoped that the appointment will be kept, for she has hurried Richard Henry past all sorts of wonderful things which he wanted to stop with for a little. But the thought of this lovely crab, which Jenny thinks so much of, forbids protest. Quite right not to keep it waiting. What will it be like? Will it be bigger than the sea?

We have reached the rendezvous. We see now that we need not have been in such a hurry.

"There!" says Jenny excitedly. "Isn't he a darling little crab? He's asleep." (That's why we need not have hurried.)

Richard Henry says nothing. He can't think of the words for what he is feeling. What he wants to say is that Jenny has let him down again. They passed a lot of these funny little things on their way here, but Jenny wouldn't stop because she was going to show him a Crab, a great, big, enormous darling little Crab — which might have been anything — and now it's only just this. No wonder the old gentleman didn't believe him.

Swindled — that's the word he wants. However, he can't think of it for the moment, so he tries something else.

"Darling little crab," he says.

They leave the dead crab there and hurry back.

"What shall I show you *now*?" says Jenny.

The Problem of Life

The noise of the retreating sea came pleasantly to us from a distance. Celia was lying on her — I never know how to put this nicely — well, she was lying face downwards on a rock and gazing into a little pool which the tide had forgotten about and left behind. I sat beside her and annoyed a limpet. Three minutes ago I had taken it suddenly by surprise and with an Herculean effort moved it an eighteenth of a millimetre westwards. My silence since then was lulling it into a false security, and in another two minutes I hoped to get a move on it again.

"Do you know," said Celia with a puzzled look on her face, "sometimes I think I'm quite an ordinary person after all."

"You aren't a little bit," I said lazily; "you're just like nobody else in the world."

"Well, of course, you had to say that."

"No, I hadn't. Lots of husbands would merely have yawned." I felt one coming and stopped it just in time. Waiting for limpets to go to sleep is drowsy work. "But why are you so morbid about yourself suddenly?"

"I don't know," she said. "Only every now and then I find myself thinking the most *obvious* thoughts."

"We all do," I answered, as I stroked my limpet gently. The noise of our conversation had roused it, but a gentle stroking motion (I am told by those to whom it has confided) will frequently cause its muscles to relax. "The great thing is not to speak to them. Still, you'd better tell me now. What is it?"

"Well," she said, her cheeks perhaps a little pinker than usual, "I was just thinking that life was very wonderful. But it's a *silly* thing to say."

"It's holiday time," I reminded her. "The need for sprinkling our remarks with thoughtful words like 'economic' and 'sporadic' is over for a bit. Let us be silly." I scratched in the rock the goal to which I was urging my limpet and took out my watch. "Three thirty-five. I shall get him there by four."

Celia was gazing at two baby fishes who played in and out a bunch of sea-weed. Above the seaweed an anemone sat fatly.

"I suppose they're all just as much alive as we are," she said thoughtfully. "They marry" — I looked at my limpet with a new interest — "and bring up families and go about their business, and it all means just as much to them as it does to us."

"My limpet's business affairs mean nothing to me," I said firmly. "I am only wrapped up in him as a sprinter."

"Aren't you going to try to move him again?"

"He's not quite ready yet. He still has his suspicions."

Celia dropped into silence. Her next question showed that she had left the pool for a moment.

"Are there any people in Mars?" she asked.

"People down here say that there aren't. A man told me the other day that he knew this for a fact. On the other hand, people in Mars know for a fact that there isn't anybody on the Earth. Probably they are both wrong."

"I should like to know a lot about things," sighed Celia. "Do you know anything about limpets?"

"Only that they stick like billy-o."

"I suppose more about them *is* known than that?"

"I suppose so. By people who have made a specialty of them. For one who has preferred to amass general knowledge rather than to specialize, it is considered enough to know that they stick like billy-o."

"You haven't specialized in anything, have you?"

"Only in wives."

Celia smiled and went on. "How do you make a specialty of limpets?"

"Well, I suppose you — er — study them. You sit down and — and watch them. Probably after dark they get up and do something. And of course, in any case, you can always dissect one and see what he's had for breakfast. One way and another you get to know things about them."

"They must have a lot of time for thinking," said Celia, regarding my limpet with her head on one side. "Tell me, how do they know that there are no men in Mars?"

I sat up with a sigh.

"Celia, you do dodge about so. I have barely brought together and classified my array of facts about things in this world, when you've dashed up to another one.

What is the connexion between Mars and limpets? If there are any limpets in Mars they are freshwater ones. In the canals."

"Oh, I just wondered," she said. "I mean" — she wrinkled her forehead in the effort to find words for her thoughts — "I'm wondering what everything means, and why we're all here, and what limpets are for, and, supposing there are people in Mars, if we're the real people whom the world was made for, or if *they* are." She stopped and added, "One evening after dinner, when we get home, you must tell me all about *everything.* "

Celia has a beautiful idea that I can explain everything to her. I suppose I must have explained a stymie or a no-ball very cleverly once.

"Well," I said, "I can tell you what limpets are for now. They're like sheep and cows and horses and pheasants and — and any other animal. They're just for *us*. At least so the wise people say."

"But we don't eat limpets."

"No, but they can amuse us. This one" — and with a sudden leap I was behind him as he dozed, and I had dashed him forward another eighteenth of a millimetre — "this one has amused *me*."

"Perhaps," said Celia thoughtfully, and I don't think it was quite a nice thing for a young woman to say, "perhaps we're only meant to amuse the people in Mars."

"Then," I said lazily, "let's hope that they *are* amused."

★ ★ ★

Ten days later the Great War began. Celia said no more on the subject, but she used to look at me curiously sometimes, and I fear that the problem of life left her more puzzled than ever. At the risk of betraying myself to her as "quite an ordinary person after all" I confess that there are times when it leaves me puzzled too.

War-Time

Armageddon

The conversation had turned, as it always does in the smoking-rooms of golf clubs, to the state of poor old England, and Porkins had summed the matter up. He had marched round in ninety-seven that morning, followed by a small child with an umbrella and an arsenal of weapons, and he felt in form with himself.

"What England wants," he said, leaning back and puffing at his cigar, — "what England wants is a war. (Another whisky and soda, waiter.) We're getting flabby. All this pampering of the poor is playing the very deuce with the country. A bit of a scrap with a foreign power would do us all the good in the world." He disposed of his whisky at a draught. "We're flabby," he repeated. "The lower classes seem to have no sense of discipline nowadays. We want a war to brace us up."

It is well understood in Olympus that Porkins must not be disappointed. What will happen to him in the next world I do not know, but it will be something extremely humorous; in this world, however, he is to have all that he wants. Accordingly the gods got to work.

In the little village of Ospovat, which is in the southeastern corner of Ruritania, there lived a maiden called Maria Strultz, who was engaged to marry Captain Tomsk.

("I fancy," said one of the gods, "that it might be rather funny if Maria jilted the Captain. I have an idea that it would please Porkins."

"Whatever has Maria —" began a very young god, but he was immediately suppressed.

"Really," said the other, "I should have thought it was sufficiently obvious. You know what these mortals are." He looked round to them all.

"Is it agreed then?"

It was agreed.)

So Maria Strultz jilted the Captain.

Now this, as you may imagine, annoyed Captain Tomsk. He commanded a frontier fort on the boundary between Ruritania and Essenland, and his chief amusement in a dull life was to play cards with the Essenland captain, who commanded the fort on the other side of the river. When Maria's letter came, he felt that the only thing to do was to drown himself; on second thoughts he decided to drown his sorrows first. He did this so successfully that at the end of the evening he was convinced that it was not Maria who had jilted him, but the Essenland captain who had jilted Maria; whereupon he rowed across the river and poured his revolver into the Essenland flag which was flying over the fort. Maria thus revenged, he went home to bed, and woke next morning with a bad headache.

("Now we're off," said the gods in Olympus.)

In Diedeldorf, the capital of Essenland, the leader-writers proceeded to remove their coats.

"The blood of every true Essenlander," said the leader-writer of the "Diedeldorf Patriot", after sending out for another pot of beer, "will boil when it hears of this fresh insult to our beloved flag, an insult which can only be wiped out with blood." Then seeing that he had two "bloods" in one sentence, he crossed the second one out, substituted "the sword," and lit a fresh cigarette. "For years Essenland has writhed under the provocations of Ruritania, but has preserved a dignified silence; this last insult is more than flesh and blood can stand." Another "blood" had got in, but it was a new sentence and he thought it might be allowed to remain. "We shall not be accused of exaggeration if we say that Essenland would lose, and rightly lose, her prestige in the eyes of Europe if she let this affront pass unnoticed. In a day she would sink from a first-rate to a fifth-rate power." But he didn't say how.

The Chancellor of Essenland, in a speech gravely applauded by both sides of the House, announced the steps he had taken. An ultimatum had been sent to Ruritania demanding an apology, an indemnity of a hundred thousand marks, and the public degradation of Captain Tomsk, whose epaulettes were to be torn off by the Commander-in-Chief of the Essenland Army in the presence of a full corps of cinematograph artists. Failing this, war would be declared.

Ruritania offered the apology, the indemnity, and the public degradation of Captain Tomsk, but urged that this last ceremony would be better performed by the

Commander-in-Chief of the Ruritanian Army; otherwise Ruritania might as well cease to be a sovereign state, for she would lose her prestige in the eyes of Europe, and sink to the level of a fifth-rate power.

There was only one possible reply to this, and Essenland made it. She invaded Ruritania.

("Aren't they wonderful?" said the gods in Olympus to each other.

"But haven't you made a mistake?" asked the very young god. "Porkins lives in England, not Essenland."

"Wait a moment," said the others.)

In the capital of Borovia the leader-writer of the "Borovian Patriot" got to work. "How does Borovia stand?" he asked. "If Essenland occupies Ruritania, can any thinking man in Borovia feel safe with the enemy at his gates?" (The Borovian peasant, earning five marks a week, would have felt no less safe than usual, but then he could hardly be described as a thinking man.) "It is vital to the prestige of Borovia that the integrity of Ruritania should be preserved. Otherwise we may resign ourselves at once to the prospect of becoming a fifth-rate power in the eyes of Europe." And in a speech, gravely applauded by all parties, the Borovian Chancellor said the same thing. So the Imperial Army was mobilized and, amidst a wonderful display of patriotic enthusiasm by those who were remaining behind, the Borovian troops marched to the front . . .

110

("And there you are," said the gods in Olympus.

"But even now —" began the very young god doubtfully.

"Silly, isn't Felicia the ally of Essenland; isn't Marksland the ally of Borovia; isn't England the ally of the ally of the ally of the Country which holds the balance of power between Marksland and Felicia?"

"But if any of them thought the whole thing stupid or unjust or —"

"Their prestige," said the gods gravely, trying not to laugh.

"Oh, I see," said the very young god.)

And when a year later the hundred-thousandth English mother woke up to read that her boy had been shot, I am afraid she shed foolish tears and thought that the world had come to an end.

Poor short-sighted creature! She didn't realize that Porkins, who had marched round in ninety-six the day before, was now thoroughly braced up.

("What babies they all are," said the very young god.)

Toby

It will save trouble if I say at once that I know nothing about horses. This will be quite apparent to you, of course, before I have finished, but I don't want you to suppose that it is not also quite apparent to me. I have no illusions on the subject; neither, I imagine, has Toby.

To me there are only two kinds of horse. Chestnuts, roans, bay rums — I know nothing of all these; I can only describe a horse simply as a nice horse or a nasty horse. Toby is a nice horse.

Toby, of course, knows much more about men than I do about horses, and no doubt he describes me professionally to his colleagues as a "flea-bitten fellow standing about eighteen hoofs"; but when he is not being technical I like to think that he sums me up to himself as a nice man. At any rate I am not allowed to wear spurs, and that must weigh with a horse a good deal.

I have no real right to Toby. The Signalling Officer's official mount is a bicycle, but a bicycle in this weather —! And there *is* Toby, and somebody must ride him, and, as I point out to the other subalterns, it would only cause jealousy if one of *them* rode him, and —"

"Why would it create more jealousy than if *you* do?" asked one of them.

"Well," I said, "you're the officer commanding platoon number —"

"Fifteen."

"Fifteen. Now, why should the officer commanding the fifteenth platoon ride a horse when the officer commanding the nineteenth —"

He reminded me that there were only sixteen platoons in a battalion. It's such a long time since I had anything to do with platoons that I forget.

"All right, we'll say the sixteenth. Why shouldn't *he* have a horse? Of all the unjust — Well, you see what recriminations it would lead to. Now I don't say I'm more valuable than a platoon-commander or more effective on a horse, but, at any rate, there aren't sixteen of me. There's only one Signalling Officer, and if there *is* a spare horse over —"

"What about the Bombing Officer?" said O.C. Platoon 15 carelessly.

I had quite forgotten the Bombing Officer. Of course he is a specialist too.

"Yes, quite so, but if you would only think a little," I said, thinking hard all the time, "you would — well, put it this way. The range of a Mills bomb is about fifty yards; the range of a field telephone is several miles. Which of us is more likely to require a horse?"

"*And* the Sniping officer?" he went on dreamily.

This annoyed me.

"You don't shoot snipe from horseback," I said sharply. "You're mixing up shooting and hunting, my lad. And in any case there are reasons, special reasons, why I ride Toby — reasons of which you know nothing."

Here are the reasons: —

1. I think I have more claim to a horse called Toby than has a contributor to "Our Feathered Friends" or whatever paper the Sniping Officer writes for.

2. When I joined the Army, Celia was inconsolable. I begged her to keep a stiff upper lip, to which she replied that she could do it better if I promised not to keep a bristly one. I pointed out that the country wanted bristles; and though, between ourselves, we might regard it as a promising face spoilt for a tradition, still discipline was discipline. And so the bristles came, and remained until the happy day when the War Office, at the risk of losing the war, made them optional. Immediately they were uprooted.

Now the Colonel has only one fault (I have been definitely promised my second star in 1927, so he won't think I am flattering him with a purpose): he likes moustaches. His own is admirable, and I have no wish for him to remove it, but I think he should be equally broad-minded about mine.

"You aren't really more beautiful without it," he said. "A moustache suits you."

"My wife doesn't think so," I said firmly. I had the War Office on my side, so I could afford to be firm.

The Colonel looked at me, and then he looked out of the window, and made the following remarkable statement.

"Toby," he said gently to himself, "doesn't like clean-shaven officers."

114

This hadn't occurred to me; I let it sink in.

"Of course," I said at last, "one must consider one's horse. I quite see that."

"With a bicycle," he said, "it's different."

And so there you have the second reason. If the Bombing Officer rode Toby, I should shave again to-morrow, and then where would the Battalion be? Ruined.

So Toby and I go off together. Up till now he has been good to me. He has bitten one Company Commander, removed another, and led the Colonel a three-mile chase across country after him, so if any misunderstanding occurs between us there will be good precedent for it. So far my only real trouble has been once when billeting.

Billeting is delightful fun. You start three hours in advance of the battalion, which means that if the battalion leaves at eight in the morning, you are up in the fresh of the day, when the birds are singing. You arrive at the village and get from the Mayor or the Town Major a list of possible hostesses. Entering the first house (labelled "Officers 5") you say, "*Vous avez un lit pour un Officier ici, n'est-ce pas? Vive la France!*" She answers, "*Pas un lit,*" and you go to the next house. "*Vous avez place pour cent hommes — oui?*" "*Non,*" says she — and so on. By-and-by the battalion arrives, and everybody surrounds you. "Where are *my* men going?" "Where is *my* billet?" "Where's 'C' Company's mess?" "Have you found anything for the Pioneers?" And so one knows what it is to be popular.

Well, the other day the Major thought he'd come with me, just to give me an idea how it ought to be done. I say nothing of the result; but for reasons connected with Toby I hope he won't come again. For in the middle of a narrow street crowded with lorries, he jumped off his horse, flung (I think that's the expression) — flung me the reins and said, "Just wait here while I see the Mayor a moment."

The Major's horse I can describe quite shortly — a nasty big black horse.

Toby I have already described as a nice horse, but he had been knee-deep in mud, inspecting huts, for nearly half an hour, and was sick of billeting.

I need not describe two-hundred-lorries-on-a-dark-evening to you.

And so, seeing that you know the constituents, I must let you imagine how they all mixed . . .

This is a beastly war. But it has its times; and when our own particular bit of the battle is over, and what is left of the battalion is marching back to rest, I doubt if, even in England (which seems very far off), you will find two people more contented with the morning than Toby and I, as we jog along together.

Common

Seated in your comfortable club, my very dear sir, or in your delightful drawing-room, madam, you may smile pityingly at the idea of a mascot saving anybody's life. "What will be, will be," you say to yourself (or in Italian to your friends), "and to suppose that a charm round the neck of a soldier will divert a German shell is ridiculous." But out there, through the crumps, things look otherwise.

Common had sat on the mantelpiece at home. An ugly little ginger dog, with a bit of red tape for his tongue and two black beads for his eyes, he viewed his limited world with an air of innocent impertinence very attractive to visitors. Common he looked and Common he was called, with a Christian name of Howard for registration. For six months he sat there, and no doubt he thought that he had seen all that there was to see of the world when the summons came which was to give him so different an outlook on life.

For that summons meant the breaking up of his home. Master was going wandering from trench to trench, Mistress from one person's house to another person's house. She no doubt would take Common with her; or perhaps she couldn't be bothered with an ugly little ginger dog, and he would be stored in some repository, boarded out in some Olympic kennel. "Or do you *possibly* think Master might —"

He looked very wistful that last morning, so wistful that Mistress couldn't bear it, and she slipped him in hastily between the revolver and the boracic powder, "Just to look after you," she said. So Common came with me to France.

His first view of the country was at Rouen, when he sat at the entrance to my tent and hooshed the early morning flies away. His next at a village behind the lines, where he met stout fellows of "D" Company and took the centre of the table at mess in the apple orchard; and moreover was introduced to a French maiden of two, with whom, at the instigation of the seconds in the business — her mother and myself — a prolonged but monotonous conversation in the French tongue ensued, Common, under suitable pressure, barking idiomatically, and the maiden, carefully prompted, replying with the native for "Bow-wow." A pretty greenwood scene beneath the apple-trees, and in any decent civilization the great adventure would have ended there. But Common knew that it was not only for this that he had been brought out, and that there was more arduous work to come.

Once more he retired to the valise, for we were making now for a vill — for a heap of bricks near the river; you may guess the river. It was about this time that I made a little rhyme for him:

There was a young puppy called Howard,
Who at fighting was rather a coward;

> He never quite ran
> When the battle began,
> But he started at once to bow-wow hard.

A good poet is supposed to be superior to the exigencies of rhyme, but I am afraid that in any case Common's reputation had to be sacrificed to them. To be lyrical over anybody called Howard Common without hinting that he — well, try for yourself. Anyhow it was a lie, as so much good poetry is.

There came a time when valises were left behind and life for a fortnight had to be sustained on a pack. One seems to want very many things, but there was no hesitation about Common's right to a place. So he came to see his first German dugout, and to get a proper understanding of this dead bleached land and the great work which awaited him there. It was to blow away shells and bullets when they came too near the master in whose pocket he sat.

In this he was successful; but I think that the feat in which he takes most pride was performed one very early summer morning. A telephone line had to be laid, and, for reasons obvious to Common, rather rapidly. It was laid safely — a mere nothing to him by this time. But when it was joined up to the telephone in the front line, then he realized that he was called upon to be not only a personal mascot, but a mascot to the battalion, and he sat himself upon the telephone and called down a blessing on that cable, so that it remained whole for two days and a night when by all the rules it should have been in a thousand pieces. "And even if I didn't *really* do it all myself," he said, "anyhow I *did* make some of the men in the trench smile a little that morning, and there wasn't so *very* much smiling going on just then, you know."

After that morning he lived in my pocket, sometimes sniffing at an empty pipe, sometimes trying to read letters from Mistress which joined him every day. We had gone North to a more gentlemanly part of the line, and his duties took but little of his time, so that anything novel, like a pair of pliers or an order from the Director of Army Signals, was always welcome. To begin with he took up rather more than his fair share of the pocket, but he rapidly thinned down. Alas! in the rigours of the campaign he also lost his voice; and his little black collar, his only kit, disappeared.

Then, just when we seemed settled for the winter, we were ordered South again. Common knew what that meant, a busy time for him. We moved down slowly, and he sampled billet after billet, but we arrived at last and sat down to wait for the day.

And then he began to get nervous. Always he was present when the operations were discussed; he had seen all the maps; he knew exactly what was expected of us. And he didn't like it.

"It's more than a fellow can do," he said; "at least to be certain of. I can blow away the shells in front and the shells from the right, but if Master's map is correct we're going to get enfiladed from the left as well, and one can't be everywhere. This wants thinking about."

120

So he dived head downwards into the deepest recesses of my pocket and abandoned himself to thought. A little later he came up with a smile . . .

Next morning I stayed in bed and the doctor came. Common looked over his shoulder as he read the thermometer.

"A hundred and four," said Common. "Golly! I hope I haven't over-done it."

He came with me to the clearing station.

"I only just blowed a germ at him," he said wistfully — "one I found in his pocket. I only just blowed it at him."

We went down to the base hospital together; we went back to England. And in the hospital in England Common suddenly saw his mistress again.

"I've brought him back, Misses," he said. "Here he is. Have I done well?"

He sits now in a little basket lined with flannel, a hero returned from the War. Round his neck he wears the regimental colours, and on his chest will be sewn whatever medal is given to those who have served faithfully on the Western Front. Seated in your comfortable club, my very dear sir, or in your delightful drawing-room, madam, you smile pityingly . . .

Or perhaps you don't.

The Ballad of Private Chad

I sing of George Augustus Chadd,
Who'd always from a baby had
A deep affection for his Dad —
In other words, his Father;
Contrariwise, the father's one
And only treasure was his son,
Yes, even when he'd gone and done
Things which annoyed him rather.

For instance, if at Christmas (say)
Or on his parent's natal day
The thoughtless lad forgot to pay
The customary greeting,
His father's visage only took
That dignified reproachful look
Which dying beetles give the cook
Above the clouds of Keating.

As years went on such looks were rare;
The younger Chadd was always there
To greet his father and to share
His father's birthday party;
The pink "For auld acquaintance sake"
Engraved in sugar on the cake
Was his. The speech he used to make
Was reverent but hearty.

The younger Chadd was twentyish
When War broke out, but did not wish
To get an A.S.C. commish
Or be a rag-time sailor;
Just Private Chadd he was, and went
To join his Dad's old regiment,
While Dad (the dear old dug-out) sent
For red tabs from the tailor.

To those inured to war's alarms
I need not dwell upon the charms
Of raw recruits when sloping arms,
Nor tell why Chadd was hoping
That, if his sloping-powers increased,
They'd give him two days' leave at least
To join his Father's birthday feast . . .
And so resumed his sloping.

One morning on the training ground,
When fixing bayonets, he found
The fatal day already round,
And, even as he fixed, he
Decided then and there to state
To Sergeant Brown (at any rate)
His longing to congratulate
His sire on being sixty.

"Sergeant," he said, "we're on the eve
Of Father's birthday; grant me leave"
(And here his bosom gave a heave)
"To offer him my blessing;
And, if a Private's tender thanks —
Nay, do not blank my blanky blanks!
I could not help but leave the ranks;
Birthdays are more than dressing."

The Sergeant was a kindly soul,
He loved his men upon the whole,
He'd also had a father's *rôle*
Pressed on him fairly lately.
"Brave Chadd," he said, "thou speakest sooth!
O happy day! O pious youth!
Great," he extemporized, "is Truth,
And it shall flourish greatly."

The Sergeant took him by the hand
And led him to the Captain, and
The Captain tried to understand,
And (more or less) succeeded;
"Correct me if you don't agree,
But one of you wants *what?*" said he,
And George Augustus Chadd said,
"Me!"
Meaning of course that *he* did.

The Captain took him by the ear
And gradually brought him near
The Colonel, who was far from clear,
But heard it all politely,
And asked him twice, "You want a
what?"
The Captain said that *he* did not,
And Chadd saluted quite a lot
And put the matter rightly.

The Colonel took him by the hair
And furtively conveyed him where
The General inhaled the air,
Immaculately booted;
Then said, "Unless I greatly err
This Private wishes to prefer
A small petition to you, Sir,"
And so again saluted.

The General inclined his head
Towards the two of them and said,
"Speak slowly, please, or shout instead;
I'm hard of hearing, rather."
So Chadd, that promising recruit,
Stood to attention, clicked his boot,
And bellowed, with his best salute,
"*A happy birthday, Father!*"

One Star

Occasionally I receive letters from friends, whom I have not seen lately, addressed to Lieutenant M — and apologizing prettily inside in case I am by now a colonel; in drawing-rooms I am sometimes called "Captain-er"; and up at the Fort the other day a sentry of the Royal Defence Corps, wearing the Crécy medal, mistook me for a Major, and presented crossbows to me. This is all wrong. As Mr. Garvin well points out, it is important that we should not have a false perspective of the War. Let me, then, make it perfectly plain — I am a Second Lieutenant.

When I first became a Second Lieutenant I was rather proud. I was a Second Lieutenant "on probation." On my right sleeve I wore a single star. So:

(on probation, of course). On my left sleeve I wore another star. So:

(also on probation).

They were good stars, none better in the service; and as we didn't like the sound of "on probation" Celia put a few stitches in them to make them more permanent.

This proved effective. Six months later I had a very pleasant note from the King telling me that the days of probation were now over, and making it clear that he and I were friends.

I was now a real Second Lieutenant. On my right sleeve I had a single star. Thus:

★

(not on probation).

On my left sleeve I also had a single star. In this manner:

★

This star also was now a fixed one.

From that time forward my thoughts dwelt naturally on promotion. There were exalted persons in the regiment called Lieutenants. They had two stars on each sleeve. So:

I decided to become a Lieutenant.

Promotion in our regiment was difficult. After giving the matter every consideration I came to the conclusion that the only way to win my second star was to save the Colonel's life. I used to follow him about affectionately in the hope that he would fall into the sea. He was a big strong man and a powerful swimmer, but once in the water it would not be difficult to cling round his neck and give an impression that I was rescuing him. However, he refused to fall in. I fancy that he wore somebody's Military Soles which prevent slipping.

Years rolled on. I used to look at my stars sometimes, one on each sleeve; they seemed very lonely. At times they came close together; but at other times as, for instance, when I was semaphoring, they were very far apart. To prevent these occasional separations Celia took them off my sleeves and put them on my shoulders. One on each shoulder. So:

★

And so:

★

There they stayed.

And more years rolled on.

One day Celia came to me in great excitement.

"Have you seen this in the paper about promotion?" she said eagerly.

"No; what is it?" I asked. "Are they making more generals?"

"I don't know about generals; it's Second Lieutenants being Lieutenants."

"You're joking on a very grave subject," I said seriously. "You can't expect to win the War if you go on like that."

"Well, you read it," she said, handing me the paper.

I took the paper with a trembling hand, and read. She was right! If the paper was to be believed, all Second Lieutenants were to become Lieutenants after eighteen years' service. At last my chance had come.

"My dear, this is wonderful," I said. "In another fifteen years we shall be there. You might buy two more stars this afternoon and practise sewing them on, in order to be ready. You mustn't be taken by surprise when the actual moment comes."

"But you're a Lieutenant *now*," she said, "if that's true. It says that 'after eighteen months —'"

I snatched up the paper again. Good Heavens! it was eighteen *months* — not years.

"Then I *am* a Lieutenant," I said.

We had a bottle of champagne for dinner that night, and Celia got the paper and read it aloud to my tunic. And just for practice she took the two stars off my other tunic and sewed them on this one — thus:

And we had a very happy evening.

"I suppose it will be a few days before it's officially announced," I said.

"Bother, I suppose it will," said Celia, and very reluctantly she took one star off each shoulder, leaving the matter — so:

And the years rolled on . . .

And I am still a Second Lieutenant . . .

I do not complain; indeed I am even rather proud of it. If I am not gaining on my original one star, at least I am keeping pace with it. I might so easily have been a corporal by now.

But I should like to have seen a little more notice taken of me in the "Gazette." I scan it every day, hoping for some such announcement as this:

"*Second Lieutenant M — to remain a Second Lieutenant.*"

Or this:

"*Second Lieutenant M — to be seconded and to retain his present rank of Second Lieutenant.*"

Or even this:

"*Second Lieutenant M — relinquishes the rank of Acting Second Lieutenant on ceasing to command a Battalion, and reverts to the rank of Second Lieutenant.*"

Failing this, I have thought sometimes of making an announcement in the Personal Column of "The Times":

"Second Lieutenant M — regrets that his duties as a Second Lieutenant prevent him from replying personally to the many kind inquiries he has received, and begs to take this opportunity of announcing that he still retains a star on each shoulder. Both doing well."

But perhaps that is unnecessary now. I think that by this time I have made it clear just how many stars I possess.

One on the right shoulder. So:

And one on the left shoulder. So:

That is all.

O.B.E.

I know a Captain of Industry,
Who made big bombs for the R.F.C.,
And collared a lot of £s.d. —
And he — thank God! — has the O.B.E.

I know a Lady of Pedigree,
Who asked some soldiers out to tea,
And said "Dear me!" and "Yes, I see" —
And she — thank God! — has the O.B.E.

I know a fellow of twenty-three,
Who got a job with a fat M.P. —
(Not caring much for the Infantry.)
And he — thank God! — has the O.B.E.

I had a friend; a friend, and he
Just held the line for you and me,
And kept the Germans from the sea,
And died — without the O.B.E.
              Thank God!
He died without the O.B.E.

The Joke: A Tragedy

CHAPTER I

The Joke was born one October day in the trench called Mechanics, not so far from Loos. We had just come back into the line after six days in reserve, and, the afternoon being quiet, I was writing my daily letter to Celia. I was telling her about our cat, imported into our dug-out in the hope that it would keep the rats down, when suddenly the Joke came. I was so surprised by it that I added in brackets, "This is quite my own. I've only just thought of it." Later on the Post-Corporal came, and the Joke started on its way to England.

CHAPTER II

Chapter II finds me some months later at home again.

"Do you remember that joke about the rats in one of your letters?" said Celia one evening.

"Yes. You never told me if you liked it."

"I simply loved it. You aren't going to waste it, are you?"

"If you simply loved it, it wasn't wasted."

"But I want everybody else — Couldn't you use it in the Revue?"

I was supposed to be writing a Revue at this time for a certain impresario. I wasn't getting on very fast, because whenever I suggested a scene to him, he either said, "Oh, that's been done," which killed it, or else he said, "Oh, but that's never been done," which killed it even more completely.

"Good idea," I said to Celia. "We'll have a Trench Scene."

I suggested it to the impresario when next I saw him.

"Oh, that's been done," he said.

"Mine will be quite different from anybody else's," I said firmly.

He brightened up a little.

"All right, try it," he said.

I seemed to have discovered the secret of successful revue-writing.

The Trench Scene was written. It was written round the Joke, whose bright beams, like a perfect jewel in a perfect setting — However, I said all that to Celia at the time. She was just going to have said it herself, she told me.

So far, so good. But a month later the Revue collapsed. The impresario and I agreed upon many things — as, for instance, that the War would be a long one, and that Hindenburg was no fool — but there were two points upon which we could never quite agree: (1) What was funny, and (2) which of us was writing the Revue. So, with mutual expressions of goodwill, and hopes that one day we might write a tragedy together, we parted.

That ended the Revue; it ended the Trench Scene; and, for the moment, it ended the Joke.

CHAPTER III

Chapter III finds the war over and Celia still at it.

"You haven't got that Joke in yet."

She had just read an article of mine called "Autumn in a Country Vicarage."

"It wouldn't go in there very well," I said.

"It would go in anywhere where there were rats. There might easily be rats in a vicarage."

"Not in this one."

"You talk about 'poor as a church mouse.'"

"I am an artist," I said, thumping my heart and forehead and other seats of the emotions. "I don't happen to see rats there, and if I don't see them I can't write about them. Anyhow, they wouldn't be secular rats, like the ones I made my joke about."

"I don't mind whether the rats are secular or circular," said Celia, "but do get them in soon."

Well, I tried. I really did try, but for months I couldn't get those rats in. It was a near thing sometimes, and I would think that I had them, but at the last moment they would whisk off and back into their holes again. I even wrote an article about "Cooking in the Great War," feeling that that would surely tempt them, but they were not to be drawn . . .

CHAPTER IV

But at last the perfect opportunity came. I received a letter from a botanical paper asking for an article on the Flora of Trench Life.

"Hooray!" said Celia. "There you are."

I sat down and wrote the article. Working up gradually to the subject of rats, and even more gradually intertwining it, so to speak, with the subject of cats, I brought off in one perfect climax the great Joke.

"Lovely!" said Celia excitedly.

"There is one small point which has occurred to me. Rats are *fauna*, not *flora*; I've just remembered."

"Oh, does it matter?"

"For a botanical paper, yes."

And then Celia had a brilliant inspiration.

"Send it to another paper," she said.

I did. Two days later it appeared. Considering that I hadn't had a proof, it came out extraordinarily well. There was only one misprint. It was at the critical word of the Joke

CHAPTER V

"That's torn it," I said to Celia.

"I suppose it has," she said sadly.

"The world will never hear the Joke now. It's had it wrong, but still it's had it, and I can't repeat it."

Celia began to smile.

"It's sickening," she said; "but it's really rather funny, you know."

And then she had another brilliant inspiration.

"In fact you might write an article about it."

And, as you see, I have.

EPILOGUE

Having read thus far, Celia says, "But you still haven't got the Joke in."

Oh, well, here goes.

Extract from letter: "We came back to the line to-day to find that the cat had kittened. However, as all the rats seem to have rottened we are much as we were."

"Rottened" was misprinted "rattened," which seems to me to spoil the Joke . . .

Yet I must confess that there are times now when I feel that perhaps after all I may have overrated it . . .

But it was a pleasant joke in its day.

Home Notes

The Way Down

Sydney Smith, or Napoleon or Marcus Aurelius (somebody about that time) said that after ten days any letter would answer itself. You see what he meant. Left to itself your invitation from the Duchess to lunch next Tuesday is no longer a matter to worry about by Wednesday morning. You were either there or not there; it is unnecessary to write now and say that a previous invitation from the Prime Minister — and so on. It was Napoleon's idea (or Dr. Johnson's or Mark Antony's — one of that circle) that all correspondence can be treated in this manner.

I have followed these early Masters (or whichever one it was) to the best of my ability. At any given moment in the last few years there have been ten letters that I absolutely *must* write, thirty which I *ought* to write, and fifty which any other person in my position *would* have written. Probably I have written two. After all, when your profession is writing, you have some excuse for demanding a change of occupation in your leisure hours. No doubt if I were a coal-heaver by day, my wife would see to the fire after dinner while I wrote letters. As it is, she does the correspondence, while I gaze into the fire and think about things.

You will say, no doubt, that this was all very well before the War, but that in the Army a little writing would be a pleasant change after the day's duties. Allow me to disillusion you. If, years ago, I had ever conceived a glorious future in which my autograph might be of value to the more promiscuous collectors, that conception has now been shattered. Four years in the Army has absolutely spoilt the market. Even were I revered in the year 2000 A.D. as Shakespeare is revered now, my half-million autographs, scattered so lavishly on charge-sheets, passes, chits, requisitions, indents and applications would keep the price at a dead level of about ten a penny. No, I have had enough of writing in the Army and I never want to sign my own name again. "Yours sincerely, Herbert Asquith," "Faithfully yours, J. Jellicoe" — these by all means; but not my own.

However, I wrote a letter in the third year of the war; it was to the bank. It informed the Manager that I had arrived in London from France and should be troubling them again shortly, London being to all appearances an expensive place. It also called attention to my new address — a small furnished flat in which Celia and I could just turn round if we did it separately. When it was written, then came the question of posting it. I was all for waiting till the next morning, but Celia explained that there was actually a letterbox on our own floor, twenty yards down the passage. I took the letter along and dropped it into the slit.

Then a wonderful thing happened. It went

Flipperty — *flipperty* — *flipperty* — *flipperty* — *flipperty* — *flipperty* — *flipperty* — *flipperty* — *flipperty* — *flipperty* — *FLOP*.

142

I listened intently, hoping for more . . . but that was all. Deeply disappointed that it was over, but absolutely thrilled with my discovery, I hurried back to Celia.

"Any letters you want posted?" I said in an off-hand way.

"No, thank you," she said.

"Have you written any while we've been here?"

"I don't think I've had anything to write."

"I think," I said reproachfully, "it's quite time you wrote to your — your bank or your mother or somebody."

She looked at me and seemed to be struggling for words.

"I know exactly what you're going to say," I said, "but don't say it; write a little letter instead."

"Well, as a matter of fact I *must* just write a note to the laundress."

"To the laundress," I said. "Of course, just a note."

When it was written I insisted on her coming with me to post it. With great generosity I allowed her to place it in the slit. A delightful thing happened. It went *Flipperty — flipperty — flipperty — flipperty — flipperty — flipperty — flipperty — flipperty — flipperty — flipperty — FLOP.*

Right down to the letter-box in the hall. Two flipperties a floor. (A simple calculation shows that we are perched on the fifth floor. I am glad now that we live so high. It must be very dull to be on the fourth floor with only eight flipperties, unbearable to be on the first with only two.)

"*O-oh!* How *fas*-cinating!" said Celia.

"Now don't you think you ought to write to your mother?"

"Oh, I *must*."

She wrote. We posted it. It went.

Flipperty — flipperty — However, you know all about that now.

Since this great discovery of mine, life has been a more pleasurable business. We feel now that there are romantic possibilities about Letters setting forth on their journey from our floor. To start life with so many flipperties might lead to anything. Each time that we send a letter off we listen in a tremble of excitement for the final FLOP, and when it comes I think we both feel vaguely that we are still waiting for something. We are waiting to hear some magic letter go *flipperty — flipperty — flipperty — flipperty* . . . and behold! there is no FLOP . . . and still it goes on — *flipperty — flipperty — flipperty — flipperty —* growing fainter in the distance . . . until it arrives at some wonderland of its own. One day it must happen so. For we cannot listen always for that *FLOP*, and hear it always; nothing in this world is as inevitable as that. One day we shall look at each other with awe in our faces and say, "But it's still flipperting!" and from that time forward the Hill of Campden will be a place holy and enchanted. Perhaps on Midsummer Eve —

At any rate I am sure that it is the only way in which to post a letter to Father Christmas.

Well, what I want to say is this: if I have been a bad correspondent in the past I am a good one now; and Celia, who was always a good one, is a better one. It takes at least ten letters a day to satisfy us, and we prefer to catch ten different posts. With the ten in your hand together there is always a temptation to waste them in one wild rush of flipperties, all catching each other up. It would be a great moment, but I do not think we can afford it yet; we must wait until we get more practised at letter-writing. And even then I am doubtful; for it might be that, lost in the confusion of that one wild rush, the magic letter would start on its way — *flipperty* — *flipperty* — to the never-land, and we should forever have missed it.

So, friends, acquaintances, yes, and even strangers, I beg you now to give me another chance. I will answer your letters, how gladly. I still think that Napoleon (or Canute or the younger Pliny — one of the pre-Raphaelites) took a perfectly correct view of his correspondence . . . but then *he* never had a letter-box which went

Flipperty — *flipperty* — *flipperty* — *flipperty* — *flipperty* — *flipperty* — *flipperty* — *flipperty* — *flipperty* — *flipperty* — *FLOP*.

Heavy Work

Every now and then doctors slap me about and ask me if I was always as thin as this.

"As thin as what?" I say with as much dignity as is possible to a man who has had his shirt taken away from him.

"As thin as this," says the doctor, hooking his stethoscope on to one of my ribs, and then going round to the other side to see how I am getting on there.

I am slightly better on the other side, but he runs his pencil up and down me and produces that pleasing noise which small boys get by dragging a stick along railings.

I explain that I was always delicately slender, but that latterly my ribs have been overdoing it.

"You must put on more flesh," he says sternly, running his pencil up and down them again. (He must have been a great nuisance as a small boy.)

"I will," I say fervently, "I will."

Satisfied by my promise he gives me back my shirt.

But it is not only the doctor who complains; Celia is even more upset by it. She says tearfully that I remind her of a herring. Unfortunately she does not like herrings. It is my hope some day to remind her of a turbot and make her happy. She, too, has my promise that I will put on flesh.

We had a fortnight's leave a little while ago, which seemed to give me a good opportunity of putting some on. So we retired to a house in the country where there is a weighing-machine in the bathroom. We felt that the mere sight of this weighing-machine twice daily would stimulate the gaps between my ribs. They would realize that they had been brought down there on business.

The first morning I weighed myself just before stepping into the water. When I got down to breakfast I told Celia the result.

"You *are* a herring," she said sadly.

"But think what an opportunity it gives me. If I started the right weight, the rest of the fortnight would be practically wasted. By the way, the doctor talks about putting on flesh, but he didn't say how much he wanted. What do you think would be a nice amount?"

"About another stone," said Celia. "You were just a nice size before the War."

"All right. Perhaps I had better tell the weighing-machine. This is a co-operative job; I can't do it all myself."

The next morning I was the same as before, and the next, and the next, and the next.

"Really," said Celia, pathetically, "we might just as well have gone to a house where there wasn't a weighing-machine at all. I don't believe it's trying. Are you sure you stand on it long enough?"

"Long enough for me. It's a bit cold, you know."

"Well, make quite sure to-morrow. I must have you not quite so herringy."

I made quite sure the next morning. I had eight stone and a half on the weight part, and the-little-thing-you-move-up-and-down was on the "4" notch, and the bar balanced midway between the top and the bottom. To have had a crowd in to see would have been quite unnecessary; the whole machine was shouting eight-stone-eleven as loudly as it could.

"I expect it's got used to you," said Celia when I told her the sad state of affairs. "It likes eight-stone-eleven people."

"We will give it," I said, "one more chance."

Next morning the weights were as I had left them, and I stepped on without much hope, expecting that the bar would come slowly up to its midway position of rest. To my immense delight, however, it never hesitated but went straight up to the top. At last I had put on flesh!

Very delicately I moved the-thing-you-move-up-and-down to its next notch. Still the bar stayed at the top. I had put on at least another ounce of flesh!

I continued to put on more ounces. Still the bar remained up! I was eight-stone-thirteen . . . Good heavens, I was eight-stone-fourteen!

I pushed the-thing-you-move-up-and-down back to the zero position, and exchanged the half-stone weight for a stone one. Excited but a trifle cold, for it was a fresh morning, and the upper part of the window was wide open, I went up from nine stone ounce by ounce . . .

At nine-stone-twelve I jumped off for a moment and shut the window . . .

At eleven-stone-eight I had to get off again in order to attend to the bath, which was in danger of overflowing . . .

At fifteen-stone-eleven the breakfast gong went . . .

At nineteen-stone-nine I realized that I had overdone it. However I decided to know the worst. The worst that the machine could tell me was twenty-stone-seven. At twenty-stone-seven I left it.

Celia, who had nearly finished breakfast, looked up eagerly as I came in.

"Well?" she said.

"I am sorry I am late," I apologized, "but I have been putting on flesh."

"Have you really gone up?" she asked excitedly.

"Yes." I began mechanically to help myself to porridge, and then stopped.

"No, perhaps not," I said thoughtfully.

"Have you gone up much?"

"Much," I said. "Quite much."

"How much? Quick!"

"Celia," I said sadly, "I am twenty-stone-seven. I may be more; the weighing-machine gave out then."

"Oh, but, darling, that's much too much."

"Still, it's what we came here for," I pointed out. "No, no bacon, thanks; a small piece of dry toast."

"I suppose the machine couldn't have made a mistake?"

"It seemed very decided about it. It didn't hesitate at all."

"Just try again after breakfast to make sure."

"Perhaps I'd better try now," I said, getting up, "because if I turned out to be only twenty-stone-six I might venture on a little porridge after all. I shan't be long."

I went upstairs. I didn't dare face that weighing-machine in my clothes after the way in which I had already strained it without them. I took them off hurriedly and stepped on. To my joy the bar stayed in its downward position. I took off an ounce . . . then another ounce. The bar remained down . . .

At eighteen-stone-two I jumped off for a moment in order to shut the window, which some careless housemaid had opened again . . .

At twelve-stone-seven I shouted through the door to Celia that I shouldn't be long, and that I should want the porridge after all . . .

At four-stone-six I said that I had better have an egg or two as well.

At three ounces I stepped off, feeling rather shaken.

I have not used the weighing-machine since; partly because I do not believe it is trustworthy, partly because I spent the rest of my leave in bed with a severe cold. We are now in London again, where I am putting on flesh. At least the doctor who slapped me about yesterday said that I must, and I promised him that I would.

A Question of Light

As soon as Celia had got a cheque-book of her own (and I had explained the mysteries of "— & Co." to her), she looked round for a safe investment of her balance, which amounted to several pounds. My offers, first of an old stocking and afterwards of mines, mortgages and aerated breads, were rejected at once.

"I'll leave a little in the bank in case of accidents," she said, "and the rest must go somewhere absolutely safe and earn me five per cent. Otherwise they shan't have it."

We did what we could for her; we offered the money to archdeacons and other men of pronounced probity; and finally we invested it in the Blanktown Electric Light Company. Blanktown is not its real name, of course; but I do not like to let out any information which may be of value to Celia's enemies — the wicked ones who are trying to snatch her little fortune from her. The world, we feel, is a dangerous place for a young woman with money.

"Can't I *possibly* lose it now?" she asked.

"Only in two ways," I said. "Blanktown might disappear in the night, or the inhabitants might give up using electric light."

It seemed safe enough. At the same time we watched the newspapers anxiously for details of the latest inventions; and anybody who happened to mention when dining with us that he was experimenting with a new and powerful illuminant was handed his hat at once.

You have Blanktown, then, as the depository of Celia's fortune. Now it comes on the scene in another guise. I made the announcement with some pride at breakfast yesterday.

"My dear," I said, "I have been asked to deliver a lecture."

"Whatever on?" asked Celia.

"Anything I like. The last person lectured on 'The Minor Satellites of Jupiter,' and the one who comes after me is doing 'The Architecture of the Byzantine Period,' so I can take something in between."

"Like 'Frostbites,' " said Celia helpfully. "But I don't quite understand. Where is it, and why?"

"The Blanktown Literary and Philosophical Society asked me to lecture to them at Blanktown. The man who was coming is ill."

"But why *you* particularly?"

"One comes down to me in the end," I said modestly.

"I expect it's because of my electric lights. Do they give you any money for it?"

"They asked me to name my fee."

"Then say a thousand pounds, and lecture on the need for more electric light. Fancy if I got six per cent!"

"This is a very sordid conversation," I said. "If I agree to lecture at all, it will be simply because I feel that I have a message to deliver ... I will now retire into the library and consider what that message is to be."

I placed the encyclopaedia handy and sat down at my desk. I had already grasped the fact that the title of my discourse was the important thing. In the list of the Society's lectures sent to me there was hardly one whose title did not impress the imagination in advance. I must be equally impressive . . .

After a little thought I began to write.

"WASPS AND THEIR YOUNG

"*Lecture delivered before the Blanktown Literary and Philosophical Society, Tuesday, December 8th.*

"*Ladies and Gentlemen —*"

"Well," said Celia, drifting in, "how's it going?"

I showed her how far I had got.

"I thought you always began, 'My Lord Mayor, Ladies and Gentlemen,' " she said.

"Only if the Lord Mayor's there."

"But how will you know?"

"Yes, that's rather awkward. I shall have to ask the Secretary beforehand."

I began again.

"WASPS AND THEIR YOUNG

"*Lecture delivered, etc . . .*

"*My Lord Mayor, my Lords, Ladies and Gentlemen —*"

It looked much better.

"What about Baronets?" said Celia. "There's sure to be lots."

"Yes, this is going to be difficult. I shall have to have a long talk with the Secretary . . . How's this? — 'My

Lord Mayor, Lords, Baronets, Ladies and Gentlemen and Sundries.' That's got in everybody."

"That's all right. And I wanted to ask you: Have you got any lantern slides?"

"They're not necessary."

"But they're much more fun. Perhaps they'll have some old ones of Vesuvius you can work in. Well, good-bye." And she drifted out.

I went on thinking.

"No," I said to myself, "I'm on the wrong tack." So I began again: —

"SOME YORKSHIRE POT-HOLES

"*Lecture delivered before the Blanktown Literary and Philosophical Society, Tuesday, December 8th.*

"*My Lord Mayor, my Lords —*"

"I don't want to interrupt," said Celia coming in suddenly, "but — oh, what's a pot-hole?"

"A curious underground cavern sometimes found in the North."

"Aren't caverns always underground? But you're busy. Will you be in for lunch?"

"I shall be writing my lecture all day," I said busily.

At lunch I decided to have a little financial talk with Celia.

"What I feel is this," I said. "At most I can ask ten guineas for my lecture. Now my expense all the way to the North, with a night at an hotel, will be at least five pounds."

"Five-pounds-ten profit," said Celia. "Not bad."

"Ah, but wait. I have never spoken in public before. In an immense hall, whose acoustics —"

"Who are they?"

"Well, never mind. What I mean is that I shall want some elocution lessons. Say five, at a guinea each."

"That still leaves five shillings."

"If only it left that, it might be worth it. But there's a new white waistcoat. An audience soon gets tired of a lecture, and then there's nothing for the wakeful ones to concentrate on but the white waistcoat of the lecturer. It must be of a virgin whiteness. Say thirty-five shillings. So I lose thirty shillings by it. Can I afford so much?"

"But you gain the acoustics and the waistcoat."

"True. Of course, if you insist —"

"Oh, you *must*," said Celia.

So I returned to the library. By tea-time I had got as far as this: —

"ADVENTURES WITH A CAMERA IN SOMALILAND

"*Lecture delivered before the Blanktown Literary and Philo —*"

And then I had an idea. This time a brilliant one.

"Celia," I said at tea, "I have been wondering whether I ought to take advantage of your generosity."

"What generosity?"

"In letting me deliver this lecture."

"It isn't generosity, it's swank. I want to be able to tell everybody."

"Ah, but the sacrifices you are making."

"Am I?" said Celia, with interest.

"Of course you are. Consider. I ask a fee of ten guineas. They cannot possibly charge more than a shilling a head to listen to me. It would be robbery. So that if there is to be a profit at all, as presumably they anticipate, I shall have a gate of at least two hundred and fifty."

"I should *hope* so."

"Two hundred and fifty. And what does that mean? It means that at seven-thirty o'clock on the night of December the 8th two hundred and fifty residents of Blanktown will *turn out the electric lights in their drawing-rooms* . . . PERHAPS EVEN IN THEIR HALLS . . . and proceed to the lecture-room. True, the lecture-room will be lit up — a small compensation — but not for long. When the slides of Vesuvius are thrown upon the screen —"

Celia was going pale.

"But if it's not you," she faltered, "it will be somebody else."

"No; if I refuse, it will be too late then to get a substitute. Besides, they must have tried everybody else before they got down to me . . . Celia it is noble of you to sacrifice —"

"Don't go!" she cried in anguish.

I gave a deep sigh.

"For your sake," I said, "I won't."

So that settles it. If my lecture on "First Principles in Homoeopathy" is ever to be delivered, it must be delivered elsewhere.

Enter Bingo

Before I introduce Bingo I must say a word for Humphrey, his sparring partner. Humphrey found himself on the top of my stocking last December, put there, I fancy, by Celia, though she says it was Father Christmas. He is a small yellow dog, with glass optics, and the label round his neck said, "His eyes move." When I had finished the oranges and sweets and nuts, when Celia and I had pulled the crackers, Humphrey remained over to sit on the music-stool, with the air of one playing the pianola. In this position he found his uses. There are times when a husband may legitimately be annoyed; at these times it was pleasant to kick Humphrey off his stool on to the divan, to stand on the divan and kick him on to the sofa, to stand on the sofa and kick him on to the bookcase; and then, feeling another man, to replace him on the music-stool and apologize to Celia. It was thus that he lost his tail.

Here we say good-bye to Humphrey for the present; Bingo claims our attention. Bingo arrived as an absurd little black tub of puppiness, warranted (by a pedigree as long as your arm) to grow into a Pekinese. It was Celia's idea to call him Bingo; because (a ridiculous reason) as a child she had had a poodle called Bingo. The less said about poodles the better; why rake up the past?

"If there is the slightest chance of Bingo — of this animal growing up into a poodle," I said, "he leaves my house at once."

"*My* poodle," said Celia, "was a lovely dog."

(Of course, she was only a child then. She wouldn't know.)

"The point is this," I said firmly, "our puppy is meant for a Pekinese — the pedigree says so. From the look of him it will be touch and go whether he pulls it off. To call him by the name of a late poodle may just be the deciding factor. Now I hate poodles; I hate pet dogs. A Pekinese is not a pet dog; he is an undersized lion. Our puppy may grow into a small lion, or a mastiff, or anything like that; but I will *not* have him a poodle. If we call him Bingo, will you promise never to mention in his presence that you once had a — a — you know what I mean — called Bingo?"

She promised. I have forgiven her for having once loved a poodle. I beg you to forget about it. There is now only one Bingo, and he is a Pekinese puppy.

However, after we had decided to call him Bingo, a difficulty arose. Bingo's pedigree is full of names like Li Hung Chang and Sun Yat Sen; had we chosen a sufficiently Chinese name for him? Apart from what was due to his ancestors, were we encouraging him enough to grow into a Pekinese? What was there Oriental about "Bingo"?

In itself, apparently, little. And Bingo himself must have felt this; for his tail continued to be nothing but a rat's tail, and his body to be nothing but a fat tub, and his head to be almost the head of any little puppy in the world. He felt it deeply. When I ragged him about it he tried to eat my ankles. I had only to go into the room in which he was, and murmur, "Rat's tail," to myself, or (more offensive still) "Chewed string," for him to rush at me. "Where, O Bingo, is that delicate feather curling gracefully over the back, which was the pride and glory of thy great-grandfather? Is the caudal affix of the rodent thy apology for it?" And Bingo would whimper with shame.

Then we began to look him up in the map.

I found a Chinese town called "Ning-po," which strikes me as very much like "Bing-go," and Celia found another one called "Yung-Ping," which might just as well be "Yung-Bing," the obvious name of Bingo's heir when he has one. These facts being communicated to Bingo, his nose immediately began to go back a little and his tub to develop something of a waist. But what finally decided him was a discovery of mine made only yesterday. *There is a Japanese province called Bingo*. Japanese, not Chinese, it is true; but at least it is Oriental. In any case conceive one's pride in realizing suddenly that one has been called after a province and not after a poodle. It has determined Bingo unalterably to grow up in the right way.

You have Bingo now definitely a Pekinese. That being so, I may refer to his ancestors, always an object of veneration among these Easterns. I speak of (hats off, please!) Ch. Goodwood Lo.

Of course you know (I didn't myself till last week) that "Ch." stands for "Champion." On the male side

Champion Goodwood Lo is Bingo's great-great-grandfather. On the female side the same animal is Bingo's great-grandfather. One couldn't be a poodle after that. A fortnight after Bingo came to us we found in a Pekinese book a photograph of Goodwood Lo. How proud we all were! Then we saw above it, "Celebrities of the Past. The Late —"

Champion Goodwood Lo was no more! In one moment Bingo had lost both his great-grandfather and his great-great-grandfather!

We broke it to him as gently as possible, but the double shock was too much, and he passed the evening in acute depression. Annoyed with my tactlessness in letting him know anything about it, I kicked Humphrey off his stool. Humphrey, I forgot to say, has a squeak if kicked in the right place. He squeaked.

Bingo, at that time still uncertain of his destiny, had at least the courage of the lion. Just for a moment he hesitated. Then with a pounce he was upon Humphrey.

Till then I had regarded Humphrey — save for his power of rolling the eyes and his habit of taking long jumps from the music-stool to the bookcase — as rather a sedentary character. But in the fight which followed he put up an amazingly good resistance. At one time he was underneath Bingo; the next moment he had Bingo down; first one, then the other, seemed to gain the advantage. But blood will tell. Humphrey's ancestry is unknown; I blush to say that it may possibly be German. Bingo had Goodwood Lo to support him — in two places. Gradually he got the upper hand; and at last, taking the reluctant Humphrey by the ear, he dragged him laboriously beneath the sofa. He emerged alone, with tail wagging, and was taken on to his mistress's lap. There he slept, his grief forgotten.

So Humphrey was found a job. Whenever Bingo wants exercise, Humphrey plants himself in the middle of the room, his eyes cast upwards in an affectation of innocence. "I'm just sitting here," says Humphrey; "I believe there's a fly on the ceiling." It is a challenge which no great-grandson of Goodwood Lo could resist. With a rush Bingo is at him.

"I'll learn you to stand in my way," he splutters. And the great dust-up begins . . .

Brave little Bingo! I don't wonder that so warlike a race as the Japanese has called a province after him.

A Warm Half-Hour

Whatever the papers say, it was the hottest afternoon of the year. At six-thirty I had just finished dressing after my third cold bath since lunch, when Celia tapped on the door.

"I want you to do something for me," she said. "It's a shame to ask you on a day like this."

"It *is* rather a shame," I agreed, "but I can always refuse."

"Oh, but you mustn't. We haven't got any ice, and the Thompsons are coming to dinner. Do you think you could go and buy threepennyworth? Jane's busy, and I'm busy, and —"

"And I'm busy," I said, opening and shutting a drawer with great rapidity.

"Just threepennyworth," she pleaded. "Nice cool ice. Think of sliding home on it."

Well, of course it had to be done. I took my hat and staggered out. On an ordinary cool day it is about half a mile to the fishmonger; to-day it was about two miles and a quarter. I arrived exhausted, and with only just strength enough to kneel down and press my forehead against the large block of ice in the middle of the shop, round which the lobsters nestled.

"Here, you mustn't do that," said the fishmonger, waving me away.

I got up, slightly refreshed.

"I want," I said, "some —" and then a thought occurred to me.

After all, *did* fishmongers sell ice? Probably the large block in front of me was just a trade sign like the coloured bottles at the chemist's. Suppose I said to a fellow of the Pharmaceutical Society, "I want some of that green stuff in the window," he would only laugh. The tactful thing to do would be to buy a pint or two of laudanum first, and *then*, having established pleasant relations, ask him as a friend to lend me his green bottle for a bit.

So I said to the fishmonger, "I want some — some nice lobsters."

"How many would you like?"

"One," I said.

We selected a nice one between us, and he wrapped a piece of "Daily Mail" round it, leaving only the whiskers visible, and gave it to me. The ice being now broken — I mean the ice being now — well, you see what I mean — I was now in a position to ask for some of his ice.

"I wonder if you could let me have a little piece of your ice," I ventured.

"How much ice do you want?" he said promptly.

"Sixpennyworth," I said, feeling suddenly that Celia's threepennyworth sounded rather paltry.

"Six of ice, Bill," he shouted to an inferior at the back, and Bill tottered up with a block about the size of one of the lions in Trafalgar Square. He wrapped a piece of "Daily News" round it and gave it to me.

"Is that all?" asked the fishmonger.

"That is all," I said faintly; and, with Algernon, the overwhiskered crustacean, firmly clutched in the right hand and Stonehenge supported on the palm of the left hand, I retired.

The flat seemed a very long way away, but having bought twice as much ice as I wanted, and an entirely unnecessary lobster, I was not going to waste still more money in taxis. Hot though it was, I would walk.

For some miles all went well. Then the ice began to drip through the paper, and in a little while, the underneath part of "The Daily News" had disappeared altogether. Tucking the lobster under my arm I turned the block over, so that it rested on another part of the paper. Soon that had dissolved too. By the time I had got half-way our Radical contemporary had been entirely eaten.

Fortunately "The Daily Mail" remained. But to get it I had to disentangle Algernon first, and I had no hand available. There was only one thing to do. I put the block of ice down on the pavement, unwrapped the lobster, put the lobster next to the ice, spread its "Daily Mail" out, lifted the ice on to the paper, and — looked up and saw Mrs. Thompson approaching.

She was the last person I wanted at that moment. In an hour and a half she would be dining with us. Algernon would not be dining with us. If Algernon and Mrs. Thompson were to meet now, would she not be expecting him to turn up at every course? Think of the long drawn-out disappointment for her; not even lobster sauce!

There was no time to lose. I decided to abandon the ice. Leaving it on the pavement I clutched the lobster and walked hastily back the way I had come.

By the time I had shaken off Mrs. Thompson I was almost at the fishmonger's. That decided me. I would begin all over again, and would do it properly this time. "I want three of ice," I said with an air.

"Three of ice, Bill," said the fishmonger, and Bill gave me quite a respectable segment in "The Morning Post."

"And I want a taxi," I said, and I waved my lobster at one.

We drove quickly home.

But as we neared the flat I suddenly became nervous about Algernon. I could not take him, red and undraped, past the hall-porter, past all the other residents who might spring out at me on the stairs. Accordingly, I placed the block of ice on the seat, took off some of its "Morning Post," and wrapped Algernon up decently. Then I sprang out, gave the man a coin, and hastened into the building.

"Bless you," said Celia, "have you got it? How sweet of you!" And she took my parcel from me. "Now we shall be able — Why, what's this?"

I looked at it closely.

"It's — it's a lobster," I said. "Didn't you say lobster?"

"I said ice."

"Oh," I said, "oh, I didn't understand. I thought you said lobster."

"You can't put lobster in a cider cup," said Celia severely.

Of course I quite see that. It was foolish of me. However, it's pleasant to think that the taxi must have been nice and cool for the next man.

Wrongly Attributed

You've heard of Willy Ferrero, the Boy Conductor? A musical prodigy, seven years old, who will order the fifth oboe out of the Albert Hall as soon as look at him. Well, he has a rival.

Willy, as perhaps you know, does not play any instrument himself; he only conducts. His rival (Johnny, as I think of him) does not conduct as yet; at least, not audibly. His line is the actual manipulation of the pianoforte — the Paderewski touch. Johnny lives in the flat below, and I hear him touching.

On certain mornings in the week — no need to specify them — I enter my library and give myself up to literary composition. On the same mornings little Johnny enters his music-room (underneath) and gives himself up to musical composition. Thus we are at work together.

The worst of literary composition is this: that when you have got hold of what you feel is a really powerful idea, you find suddenly that you have been forestalled by some earlier writer — Sophocles or Shakespeare or George R. Sims. Then you have to think again. This frequently happens to me upstairs; and downstairs poor Johnny will find to his horror one day that his great work has already been given to the world by another — a certain Dr. John Bull.

Johnny, in fact, is discovering "God Save the King" with one finger.

As I dip my pen in the ink and begin to write, Johnny strikes up. On the first day when this happened, some three months ago, I rose from my chair and stood stiffly through the performance — an affair of some minutes, owing to a little difficulty with "Send him victorious," a line which always bothers Johnny. However, he got right through it at last, after harking back no more than twice, and I sat down to my work again. Generally speaking, "God Save the King" ends a show; it would be disloyal to play any other tune after that. Johnny quite saw this . . . and so began to play "God Save the King" again.

I hope that His Majesty, the Lord Chamberlain, the late Dr. Bull, or whoever is most concerned, will sympathize with me when I say that this time I remained seated. I have my living to earn.

From that day Johnny has interpreted Dr. John Bull's favourite composition nine times every morning. As this has been going on for three months, and as the line I mentioned has two special rehearsals to itself before coming out right, you can easily work out how many send-him-victoriouses Johnny and I have collaborated in. About two thousand.

Very well. Now, you ask yourself, why did I not send a polite note to Johnny's father asking him to restrain his little boy from over-composition, begging him not to force the child's musical genius too quickly, imploring him (in short) to lock up the piano and lose the key? What kept me from this course? The answer is

"Patriotism." Those deep feelings for his country which one man will express glibly by rising nine times during the morning at the sound of the National Anthem, another will direct to more solid uses. It was my duty, I felt, not to discourage Johnny. He was showing qualities which could not fail, when he grew up, to be of value to the nation. Loyalty, musical genius, determination, patience, industry — never before have these qualities been so finely united in a child of six. Was I to say a single word to disturb the delicate balance of such a boy's mind? At six one is extraordinarily susceptible to outside influence. A word from his father to the effect that the gentleman above was getting sick of it, and Johnny's whole life might be altered.

No, I would bear it grimly.

And then, yesterday, who should write to me but Johnny's father himself. This was the letter:

"Dear Sir — I do not wish to interfere unduly in the affairs of the other occupants of these flats, but I feel bound to call your attention to the fact that for many weeks now there has been a flow of water from your bathroom, which has penetrated through the ceiling of my bathroom, particularly after you have been using the room in the mornings. May I therefore beg you to be more careful in future not to splash or spill water on your floor, seeing that it causes inconvenience to the tenants beneath you?

"Yours faithfully, Jno. McAndrew."

You can understand how I felt about this. For months I had been suffering Johnny in silence; yet, at the first little drop of water from above, Johnny's father must break out into violent abuse of me. A fine reward! Well, Johnny's future could look after itself now; anyhow, he was doomed with a selfish father like that.

"Dear Sir," I answered defiantly, "Now that we are writing to each other I wish to call your attention to the fact that for many months past there has been a constant flow of one-fingered music from your little boy, which penetrates through the floor of my library and makes all work impossible. May I beg you, therefore, to see that your child is taught a new tune immediately, seeing that the National Anthem has lost its first freshness for the tenants above him?"

His reply to this came to-day.

"Dear Sir, — I have no child.

"Yours faithfully, Jno. McAndrew."

I was so staggered that I could only think of one adequate retort.

"DEAR SIR," I wrote, — "I never have a bath."

So that's the end of Johnny, my boy prodigy, for whom I have suffered so long. It is not Johnny but Jno. who struggles with the National Anthem. He will give up music now, for he knows I have the bulge on him; I can flood his bathroom whenever I like. Probably he will learn something quieter — like painting. Anyway, Dr. John Bull's masterpiece will rise no more through the ceiling of the flat below.

On referring to my encyclopedia, I see that, according to some authorities, "God Save the King" is "wrongly attributed" to Dr. Bull. Well, I wrongly attributed it to Johnny. It is easy to make these mistakes.

A Hanging Garden in Babylon

"Are you taking me to the Flower Show this afternoon?" asked Celia at breakfast.

"No," I said thoughtfully; "no."

"Well, that's that. What other breakfast conversation have I? Have you been to any theatres lately?"

"Do you really want to go to the Flower Show?" I asked. "Because I don't believe I could bear it."

"I've saved up two shillings."

"It isn't that — not only that. But there'll be thousands of people there, all with gardens of their own, all pointing to things and saying, 'We've got one of those in the east bed,' or 'Wouldn't that look nice in the south orchid house?' and you and I will be quite, quite out of it." I sighed, and helped myself from the west toast-rack.

It is very delightful to have a flat in London, but there are times in the summer when I long for a garden of my own. I show people round our little place, and I point out hopefully the Hot Tap Doultonii in the scullery, and the Dorothy Perkins doormat, but it isn't the same thing as taking your guest round your garden and telling him that what you really want is rain. Until

172

I can do that, the Chelsea Flower Show is no place for us.

"Then I haven't told you the good news," said Celia. "We *are* gardeners." She paused a moment for effect. "I have ordered a window-box."

I dropped the marmalade and jumped up eagerly.

"But this is glorious news! I haven't been so excited since I recognized a calceolaria last year, and told my host it was a calceolaria just before he told me. A window-box! What's in it?"

"Pink geraniums and — and pink geraniums, and — er —"

"Pink geraniums?" I suggested.

"Yes. They're very pretty, you know."

"I know. But I could have wished for something more difficult. If we had something like — well, I don't want to seem to harp on it, but say calceolarias, then quite a lot of people mightn't recognize them, and I should be able to tell them what they were. I should be able to show them the calceolarias; you can't show people the geraniums."

"You can say, 'What do you think of *that* for a geranium?' " said Celia. "Anyhow," she added, "you've got to take me to the Flower Show now."

"Of course I will. It is not only a pleasure, but a duty. As gardeners we must keep up with floricultural progress. Even though we start with pink geraniums now, we may have — er — calceolarias next year. Rotation of crops and — what not."

Accordingly we made our way in the afternoon to the Show.

"I think we're a little over-dressed," I said as we paid our shillings. "We ought to look as if we'd just run up from our little window-box in the country and were going back by the last train. I should be in gaiters, really."

"Our little window-box is not in the country," objected Celia. "It's what you might call a *pied de terre* in town. French joke," she added kindly.

"Much more difficult than the ordinary sort."

"Don't forget it; we can always use it again on visitors. Now what shall we look at first?

"The flowers first; then the tea."

I had bought a catalogue and was scanning it rapidly.

"We don't want flowers," I said. "Our window-box — our garden is already full. It may be that James, the head boxer, has overdone the pink geraniums this year, but there it is. We can sack him and promote Thomas, but the mischief is done. Luckily there are other things we want. What about a dove-cot? I should like to see doves cooing round our geraniums."

"Aren't dove-cots very big for a window-box?"

"We could get a small one — for small doves. Do you have to buy the doves too, or do they just come? I never know. Or there," I broke off suddenly; "my dear, that's just the thing." And I pointed with my stick.

"We have seven clocks already," said Celia.

"But a sun-dial! How romantic. Particularly as only two of the clocks go. Celia, if you'd let me have a sun-dial in my window-box, I would meet you by it alone sometimes."

"It sounds lovely," she said doubtfully.

"You do want to make this window-box a success, don't you?" I asked as we wandered on. "Well, then, help me to buy something for it. I don't suggest one of those," and I pointed to a summer-house, "or even a weather-cock; but we must do something now we're here. For instance, what about one of these patent extension ladders, in case the geraniums grow very tall and you want to climb up and smell them? Or would you rather have some mushroom spawn? I would get up early and pick the mushrooms for breakfast. What do you think?"

"I think it's too hot for anything, and I must sit down. Is this seat an exhibit or is it meant for sitting on?"

"It's an exhibit, but we might easily want to buy one some day, when our window-box gets bigger. Let's try it."

It was so hot that I think, if the man in charge of the Rustic Bench Section had tried to move us on, we should have bought the seat at once. But nobody bothered us. Indeed it was quite obvious that the news that we owned a large window-box had not yet got about.

"I shall leave you here," I said, after I had smoked a cigarette and dipped into the catalogue again, "and make my purchase. It will be quite inexpensive; indeed, it is marked in the catalogue at one-and-six-pence, which means that they will probably offer me the nine-shilling size first. But I shall be firm. Good-bye."

I went and bought one and returned to her with it.

"No, not now," I said, as she held out her hand eagerly. "Wait till we get home."

It was cooler now, and we wandered through the tents, chatting patronizingly to the stall-keeper whenever we came to pink geraniums. At the orchids we were contemptuously sniffy. "Of course," I said, "for those who *like* orchids —" and led the way back to the geraniums again. It was an interesting afternoon.

And to our great joy the window-box was in position when we got home again.

"Now!" I said dramatically, and I unwrapped my purchase and placed it in the middle of our new-made garden.

"Whatever —"

"A slug-trap," I explained proudly.

"But how could slugs get up here?" asked Celia in surprise.

"How do slugs get anywhere? They climb up the walls, or they come up in the lift, or they get blown about by the wind — I don't know. They can fly up if they like; but, however it be, when they do come, I mean to be ready for them."

Still, though our slug-trap will no doubt come in usefully, it is not what we really want. What we gardeners really want is rain.

Sisterly Assistance

I was talking to a very stupid man the other day. He was the stupidest man I have come across for many years. It is a hard thing to say of any man, but he appeared to me to be entirely lacking in intellect.

It was Celia who introduced me to him. She had rung up her brother at the flat where he was staying, and, finding that he was out, she gave a message for him to the porter. It was simply that he was to ring her up as soon as he came in.

"Ring up who?" said the porter. At least I suppose he did, for Celia repeated her name (and mine) very slowly and distinctly.

"Mrs. who?" said the porter, "What?" or "I can't hear," or something equally foolish.

Celia then repeated our name again.

There followed a long conversation between the two of them, the audible part of it (that is Celia's) consisting of my name given forth in a variety of intonations, in the manner of one who sings an anthem — hopefully, pathetically, dramatically, despairingly.

Up to this moment I had been rather attached to my name. True, it wants a little explaining to shopkeepers. There are certain consonants in it which require to be elided or swallowed or swivelled round the glottis, in order to give the name its proper due. But after five or six applications the shopkeeper grasps one's meaning.

Well, as I say, I was attached to my name. But after listening to Celia for five minutes I realized that there had been some horrible mistake. People weren't called that.

"Just wait a moment," I said to her rather anxiously, and picked up the telephone book. To my great relief I found that Celia was right. There *was* a person of that name living at my address.

"You're quite right," I said. "Go on."

"I wish I had married somebody called Jones," said Celia, looking up at me rather reproachfully. "No, no, not Jones," she added hastily down the telephone, and once more she repeated the unhappy name.

"It isn't my fault," I protested. "You did have a choice; I had none. Try spelling it. It spells all right."

Celia tried spelling it.

"I'm going to spell it," she announced very distinctly down the telephone. "Are you ready? . . . M . . . No, *M*. M for mother."

That gave me an idea.

"Come away," I said, seizing the telephone; "leave it to me. Now, then," I called to the porter. "Never mind about the name. Just tell him to ring up his *sister*." And I looked at Celia triumphantly.

"Ask him to ring up his mother," said the porter. "Very well, sir."

"No, not the mother. That was something else. Forget all about that mother. He's to ring up his sister . . . *sister* . . . SISTER."

"You'll have to spell it," said Celia.

"I'm going to spell it," I shouted. "Are you ready? . . . S for — for sister."

"Now you're going to muddle him," murmured Celia.

"S for sister; have you got that? . . . No, *sister*, idiot. I for idiot," I added quickly. "S for sister — this is another sister, of course. T for two. Got that? No, *two*. Two anything — two more sisters, if you like. E for — E for —" I turned helplessly to Celia: "quick, a word to begin with E! I've got him moving now. E for — quick, before his tympanum runs down."

"Er — er —" Desperately she tried to think.

"E for er," I shouted. "That'll be another sister, I expect . . . Celia, I believe we ought to spell it with an 'H.' Can't you think of a better word?"

"Enny," said Celia, having quite lost her nerve by this time.

"E for enny," I shouted. "Any anything. Any of the sisters I've been telling you about. R for — quick, Celia!"

"Rose," she said hastily.

"R for Rose," I shouted. "Rose the flower — or the sister if you like. There you are, that's the whole word. Now then, I'll just spell it to you over again . . . Celia, I want another word for E. That last was a bad one."

"Edith?"

"Good."

I took a deep breath and began.

"S for sister. I for Isabel — Isabel is the name of the sister. S for another sister — I'll tell you *her* name

180

directly. T for two sisters, these two that we're talking about. E for Edith, that's the second sister whose name I was going to tell you. R for Rose. Perhaps I ought to explain Rose. She was the sister whom these two sisters were sisters of. Got that?" I turned to Celia. "I'm going to get the sister idea into his head if I die for it."

"Just a moment, sir," said the dazed voice of the porter.

"What's the matter? Didn't I make it clear about Rose? She was the sister whom the —"

"Just hold the line a moment, sir," implored the porter. "Here's the gentleman himself coming in."

I handed the telephone to Celia. "Here he is," I said.

But I was quite sorry to go, for I was getting interested in those sisters. Rose, I think, will always be my favourite. Her life, though short, was full of incident, and there were many things about her which I could have told that porter. But perhaps he would not have appreciated them. It is a hard thing to say of any man, but he appeared to me to be entirely lacking in intellect.

The Obvious

Celia had been calling on a newly married friend of hers. They had been schoolgirls together; they had looked over the same algebra book (or whatever it was that Celia learnt at school — I have never been quite certain); they had done their calisthenics side by side; they had compared picture post cards of Lewis Waller. Ah, me! the fairy princes they had imagined together in those days . . . and here am I, and somewhere in the City (I believe he is a stockbroker) is Ermyntrude's husband, and we play our golf on Saturday afternoons, and go to sleep after dinner, and — Well, anyhow, they were both married, and Celia had been calling on Ermyntrude.

"I hope you did all the right things," I said. "Asked to see the wedding-ring, and admired the charming little house, and gave a few hints on the proper way to manage a husband."

"Rather," said Celia. "But it did seem funny, because she used to be older than me at school."

"Isn't she still?"

"Oh, no! I'm ever so much older now . . . Talking about wedding-rings," she went on, as she twisted her own round and round, "she's got all sorts of things written inside hers — the date and their initials and I don't know what else."

"There can't be much else — unless perhaps she has a very large finger."

"Well, I haven't got *anything* in mine," said Celia, mournfully. She took off the offending ring and gave it to me.

On the day when I first put the ring on her finger, Celia swore an oath that nothing but death, extreme poverty or brigands should ever remove it. I swore too. Unfortunately it fell off in the course of the afternoon, which seemed to break the spell somehow. So now it goes off and on just like any other ring. I took it from her and looked inside.

"There are all sorts of things here too," I said. "Really, you don't seem to have read your wedding-ring at all. Or, anyhow, you've been skipping."

"There's nothing," said Celia in the same mournful voice. "I do think you might have put something."

I went and sat on the arm of her chair, and held the ring up.

"You're an ungrateful wife," I said, "after all the trouble I took. Now look there," and I pointed with a pencil, "what's the first thing you see?"

"Twenty-two. That's only the —"

"That was your age when you married me. I had it put in at enormous expense. If you had been eighteen, the man said, or — or nine, it would have come much cheaper. But no, I would have your exact age. You were twenty-two and that's what I had engraved on it. Very well. Now what do you see next to it?"

"A crown."

"Yes. And what does that mean? In the language of — er — crowns it means 'You are my queen.' I insisted on a crown. It would have been cheaper to have had a lion, which means — er — lions, but I was determined not to spare myself. For I thought," I went on pathetically, "I quite thought you would like a crown."

"Oh, I do," cried Celia quickly, "if it really means that." She took the ring in her hands and looked at it lovingly. "And what's that there? Sort of a man's head."

I gazed at her sadly.

"You don't recognize it? Has a year of marriage so greatly changed me? Celia, it is your Ronald! I sat for that, hour after hour, day after day, for your sake, Celia. It is not a perfect likeness; in the small space allotted to him the sculptor has hardly done me justice. And there," I added, "is his initial 'r.' Oh, woman, the amount of thought I spent on that ring!"

She came a little closer and slipped the ring on my finger.

"Spend a little more," she pleaded. "There's plenty of room. Just have something nice written in it — something about you and me."

"Like 'Pisgah'?"

"What does that mean?"

"I don't know. Perhaps it's 'Mizpah,' or 'Ichabod,' or 'Habakkuk.' I'm sure there's a word you put on rings — I expect they'd know at the shop."

"But I don't want what they know at shops. It must be something quite private and special."

"But the shop has got to know about it when I tell them. And I don't like telling strange men in shops private and special things about ourselves. I love you, Celia, but —"

"That would be a lovely thing," she said, clasping her hands eagerly.

"What?"

" 'I love you, Celia.' "

I looked at her aghast.

"Do you want me to order that in cold blood from the shopman?"

"He wouldn't mind. Besides, if he saw us together he'd probably know. You aren't afraid of a goldsmith, are you?"

"I'm not afraid of any goldsmith living — or goldfish either, if it come to that. But I should prefer to be sentimental in some other language than plain English. I could order '*Cars sposa*,' or — or '*Spaghetti*,' or anything like that, without a tremor."

"But of course you shall put just whatever you like. Only — only let it be original. Not Mizpahs."

"Right," I said.

For three days I wandered past gold and silversmiths with the ring in my pocket . . . and for three days Celia went about without a wedding-ring, and, for all I know, without even her marriage-lines in her muff. And on the fourth day I walked boldly in.

"I want," I said, "a wedding-ring engraved," and I felt in my pockets. "Not initials," I said, and I felt in some more pockets, "but — but —" I tried the trousers pockets again. "Well, look here, I'll be quite frank with you. I — er — want —" I fumbled in my ticket-pocket,

"I want 'I love you' on it," and I went through the waistcoat pockets a third time. " 'I — er — love you.' "

"Me?" said the shopman, surprised.

"I love you," I repeated mechanically. "I love you. I love you, I — Well, look here, perhaps I'd better go back and get the ring."

On the next day I was there again; but there was a different man behind the counter.

"I want this ring engraved," I said.

"Certainly. What shall we put?"

I had felt the question coming. I had a sort of instinct that he would ask me that. But I couldn't get the words out again.

"Well," I hesitated, "I — er — well."

"Ladies often like the date put in. When is it to be?"

"When is what to be?"

"The wedding," he smiled.

"It has been," I said. "It's all over. You're too late for it."

I gave myself up to thought. At all costs I must be original. There must be something on Celia's wedding-ring that had never been in any other's . . .

There was only one thing I could think of.

The engraved ring arrived as we were at tea a few days later, and I had a sudden overwhelming fear that Celia would not be pleased. I saw that I must explain it to her. After all, there was a distinguished precedent.

"Come into the bath-room a moment," I said, and I led the way.

She followed, wondering.

"What is that?" I asked, pointing to a blue thing on the floor.

"The bath-mat," she said, surprised.

"And that is written on it?"

"Why — 'bath-mat,' of course."

"Of course," I said . . . and I handed her the wedding-ring.

A Few Guests

The Arrival of Blackman's Warbler

I have become an Authority on Birds. It happened in this way.

The other day we heard the Cuckoo in Hampshire. (The next morning the papers announced that the Cuckoo had been heard in Devonshire — possibly a different one, but in no way superior to ours except in the matter of its Press agent.) Well, everybody in the house said, "Did you hear the Cuckoo?" to everybody else, until I began to get rather tired of it; and, having told everybody several times that I *had* heard it, I tried to make the conversation more interesting. So, after my tenth "Yes," I added quite casually:

"But I haven't heard the Tufted Pipit yet. It's funny why it should be so late this year."

"Is that the same as the Tree Pipit?" said my hostess, who seemed to know more about birds than I had hoped.

"Oh, no," I said quickly.

"What's the difference exactly?"

"Well, one is tufted," I said, doing my best, "and the other — er — climbs trees."

"Oh, I see."

"And of course the eggs are more speckled," I added, gradually acquiring confidence.

"I often wish I knew more about birds," she said regretfully. "You must tell us something about them now we've got you here."

And all this because of one miserable Cuckoo!

"By all means," I said, wondering how long it would take to get a book about birds down from London.

However, it was easier than I thought. We had tea in the garden that afternoon, and a bird of some kind struck up in the plane-tree.

"There, now," said my hostess, "what's that?"

I listened with my head on one side. The bird said it again.

"That's the Lesser Bunting," I said hopefully.

"The Lesser Bunting," said an earnest-looking girl; "I shall always remember that."

I hoped she wouldn't, but I could hardly say so. Fortunately the bird lesser-bunted again, and I seized the opportunity of playing for safety.

"Or is it the Sardinian White-throat?" I wondered. "They have very much the same note during the breeding season. But of course the eggs are more speckled," I added casually.

And so on for the rest of the evening. You see how easy it is.

However, the next afternoon a more unfortunate occurrence occurred. A real Bird Authority came to tea. As soon as the information leaked out, I sent up a hasty prayer for bird-silence until we had got him safely out of the place; but it was not granted. Our feathered songster in the plane-tree broke into his little piece.

"There," said my hostess — "there's that bird again." She turned to me. "What did you say it was?"

I hoped that the Authority would speak first, and that the others would then accept my assurance that they had misunderstood me the day before; but he was entangled at that moment in a watercress sandwich, the loose ends of which were still waiting to be tucked away.

I looked anxiously at the girl who had promised to remember, in case she wanted to say something, but she also was silent. Everybody was silent except that miserable bird.

Well, I had to have another go at it. "Blackman's Warbler," I said firmly.

"Oh, yes," said my hostess.

"Blackman's Warbler; I shall always remember that," lied the earnest-looking girl.

The Authority, who was free by this time, looked at me indignantly.

"Nonsense," he said; "it's the Chiff-chaff."

Everybody else looked at me reproachfully. I was about to say that "Blackman's Warbler" was the local name for the Chiff-chaff in our part of Somerset, when the Authority spoke again.

"The Chiff-chaff," he said to our hostess with an insufferable air of knowledge.

I wasn't going to stand that.

"So *I* thought when I heard it first," I said, giving him a gentle smile. It was now the Authority's turn to get the reproachful looks.

"Are they very much alike?" my hostess asked me, much impressed.

"Very much. Blackman's Warbler is often mistaken for the Chiff-chaff, even by so-called experts" — and I turned to the Authority and added, "Have another sandwich, won't you?" — "particularly so, of course, during the breeding season. It is true that the eggs are more speckled, but —"

"Bless my soul," said the Authority, but it was easy to see that he was shaken, "I should think I know a Chiff-chaff when I hear one."

"Ah, but do you know a Blackman's Warbler? One doesn't often hear them in this country. Now in Algiers —"

The bird said "Chiff-chaff" again with an almost indecent plainness of speech.

"There you are!" I said triumphantly. "Listen," and I held up a finger. "You notice the difference? *Obviously* a Blackman's Warbler."

Everybody looked at the Authority. He was wondering how long it would take to get a book about birds down from London, and deciding that it couldn't be done that afternoon. Meanwhile he did not dare to repudiate me. For all he had caught of our mumbled introduction I might have been Blackman myself.

"Possibly you're right," he said reluctantly.

194

Another bird said "Chiff-chaff" from another tree and I thought it wise to be generous. "There," I said, "now that *was* a Chiff-chaff."

The earnest-looking girl remarked (silly creature) that it sounded just like the other one, but nobody took any notice of her. They were all busy admiring me.

Of course I mustn't meet the Authority again, because you may be pretty sure that when he got back to his books he looked up Blackman's Warbler and found that there was no such animal. But if you mix in the right society, and only see the wrong people once, it is really quite easy to be an authority on birds — or, I imagine, on anything else.

The Last Straw

It was one of those summer evenings with the chill on, so after dinner we lit the smoking-room fire and wondered what to do. There were eight of us; just the right number for two bridge tables, or four picquet pairs, or eight patience singles.

"Oh, no, not cards," said Celia quickly. "They're so dull."

"Not when you get a grand slam," said our host, thinking of an accident which had happened to him the night before.

"Even then I don't suppose anybody laughed."

Peter and I, who were partners on that occasion, admitted that we hadn't laughed.

"Well, there you are," said Celia triumphantly. "Let's play proverbs."

"I don't think I know it," said Herbert. (He wouldn't.)

"Oh, it's quite easy. First you think of a proverb."

"Like 'A burnt camel spoils the moss,' " I explained.

"You mean 'A burnt child dreads the fire,' " corrected Herbert.

Celia caught my eye and went on hurriedly, "Well, then somebody goes outside, and then he asks questions —"

"From outside?" asked Mrs. Herbert.

"From inside," I assured her. "Generally from very near the fire, because he has got so cold waiting in the hall."

"Oh, yes, I see."

"And then he asks questions, and we each have to get one of the words of the proverb into our answer, without letting him know what the proverb is. It's rather fun."

Peter and his wife, who knew the game, agreed. Mrs. Herbert seemed resigned to the worst, but Herbert, though faint, was still pursuing.

"But doesn't he *guess* what the proverb is?" he asked.

"Sometimes," I admitted. "But sometimes, if we are very, very clever, he doesn't. That, in fact, is the game."

Our host got up and went to the door.

"I think I see," he said; "and I want my pipe anyhow. So I'll go out first."

"Now then," said Celia, when the door was safely closed, "what shall we have?"

Of course you know this game, and you know the difficulty of thinking of a proverb which has no moss or stable-doors or glasshouses in it; all of them words which it is impossible to include naturally in an answer to an ordinary question. The proverbs which Mrs. Herbert suggested were full of moss.

"What about 'It's never too late to mend?' " said Mrs. Peter. "The only difficult word is 'mend.' "

"We mustn't have less than seven words, one for each of us."

"Can't we get something from Solomon for a change?" said Peter. " 'A roaring lion is a calamity to its father, but the cautious man cometh not again.' That sort of thing."

"We might try it," said Celia doubtfully, not feeling quite sure if it were a real proverb; "but 'cometh' would be difficult."

"I don't see why," said Herbert. "One could always work it in somehow."

"Well, of course, if he asked you, 'By what train cometh thou up in the mornings?' you could answer, 'I cometh up by the ten-fifteen.' Only you don't get that sort of question as a rule."

"Oh, I see," said Herbert. "I didn't quite understand."

"After all, it's really much more fun having camels and things," said Celia. "It's the last straw that breaks the camel's back.' Who'll do 'camel's'? You'd better," she added kindly to me.

Everybody but myself seemed to think that this was much more fun.

"I'll do 'straw,' " said Peter generously, whereupon Celia volunteered for "breaks." There were seven of us for nine words. We gave Mrs. Herbert the second "the," fearing to trust her with anything more alarming and in order to keep it in the family we gave the other "the" to Herbert, who was also responsible for "back." Our hostess had "last" and Mrs. Peter had "that."

All this being settled, our host was admitted into his smoking-room again.

"You begin with me," I said, and I was promptly asked, "How many blue beans make five?" When I had made a suitable answer into which "it's" came without much difficulty, our host turned to Herbert. Herbert's face had already assumed a look of strained expectancy.

"Well, Herbert, what do you think of Lloyd George?"

"Yes," said Herbert. "Yes — er — yes." He wiped the perspiration from his brow. "He — er — that is to say — er — Lloyd George, yes."

"Is that the answer?" said our host, rather surprised.

Herbert explained hastily that he hadn't really begun yet, and with the aid of an anecdote about a cousin of his who had met Winston Churchill at Dieppe once, he managed to get "the" in several times before blowing his nose vigorously and announcing that he had finished.

"I believe he's playing a different game," murmured Celia to Mrs. Peter.

The next three words were disposed of easily enough, a lucky question to Peter about the weather giving him an opportunity to refer to his straw hat. It was now Celia's turn for "breaks."

"Nervous?" I asked her.

"All of a twitter," she said.

"Well, Celia," said our host, "how long are you going to stay with us?"

"Oh, a long time yet," said Celia confidently.

"Till Wednesday, anyhow," I interrupted, thinking it a good opportunity to clinch the matter.

"We generally stay," explained Celia, "until our host breaks it to us that he can't stand us any longer."

"Not that that often happens," I added.

"Look here, which of you is answering the question?"

"I am," said Celia firmly.

"Well, have you answered it yet?"

"To tell the truth I've quite forgotten the word that — Oh, I remember now. Yes," she went on very distinctly and slowly, "I hope to remain under your roof until next Wednesday morn. Whew!" and she fanned herself with her handkerchief.

Mrs. Herbert repeated her husband's triumph with "the," and then it was my turn again for these horrible camels. My only hope was that our host would ask me if I had been to the Zoo lately, but I didn't see why he should. He didn't.

"Would it surprise you to hear," he asked, "that the President of Czecho-Slovakia has a very long beard?"

"If it had only been 'goats,' " I murmured to myself. Aloud I said, "What?" in the hope of gaining a little more time.

He repeated his question.

"No," I said slowly, "no, it wouldn't," and I telegraphed an appeal to Celia for help. She nodded back at me.

"Have you finished?" asked our host.

"Good Lord, no, I shall be half an hour yet. The fact is you've asked the wrong question. You see, I've got to get in 'moss.' "

"I thought it was 'camels,' " said Celia carelessly.

"No, 'moss.' Now if you'd only asked me a question about gardening — You see, the proverb we wanted to have first of all was 'People who live in glass houses

200

shouldn't throw stones,' only 'throw' was so difficult. Almost as difficult as —" I turned to Celia. "What was it you said just now? Oh yes, camels. Or stable doors, or frying-pans. However, there it is." And I enlarged a little more on the difficulty of getting in these difficult words.

"Thank you very much," said our host faintly when I had finished.

It was the last straw which broke the camel's back, and it was Herbert who stepped forward blithely with the last straw. Our host, as he admitted afterwards, was still quite in the dark, and with his last question he presented Herbert with an absolute gift.

"When do you go back to Devonshire?" he asked.

"We — er — return next month," answered Herbert. "I should say," he added hastily, "we go *back* next month."

My own private opinion was that the sooner he returned to Devonshire the better.

Disillusioned

The card was just an ordinary card,
The letter just an ordinary letter.
The letter simply said "Dear Mr. Brown,
I'm asked by Mrs. Phipp to send you this";
The card said, "Mrs. Philby Phipp, At Home,"
And in a corner, "Dancing, 10p.m.,"
No more — except a date, a hint in French
That a reply would not be deemed offensive,
And, most important, Mrs. Phipp's address.

Destiny, as the poets have observed
(Or will do shortly) is a mighty thing.
It takes us by the ear and lugs us firmly
Down different paths towards one common goal,
Paths pre-appointed, not of our own choosing;
Or sometimes throws two travellers together,
Marches them side by side for half a mile,
Then snatches them apart and hauls them
    onward.
Thus happened it that Mrs. Phipp and I
Had never met to any great extent,
Had never met, as far as I remembered,
At all . . . And yet there must have been a time
When she and I were very near together,

When some one told her, "*That* is Mr. Brown,"
Or introduced us "*This* is Mr. Brown,"
Or asked her if she'd heard of Mr. Brown;
I know not what, I only know that now
She stood At Home in need of Mr. Brown,
And I had pledged myself to her assistance.

Behold me on the night, the latest word
In all that separates the gentleman
(And waiters) from the evening-dress-less mob,
And graced, moreover, by the latest word
In waistcoats such as mark one from the waiters.
My shirt, I must not speak about my shirt;
My tie, I cannot dwell upon my tie —
Enough that all was neat, harmonious,
And suitable to Mrs. Philby Phipp.
Behold me, then, complete. A hasty search
To find the card, and reassure myself
That this is certainly the day — (It is) —
And 10p.m. the hour; "p.m.," not "a.m.,"
Not after breakfast — good; and then outside,

To jump into a cab and take the winds,
The cold east winds of March, with beauty. So.

Let us get on more quickly. Looms ahead
Tragedy. Let us on and have it over.

I hung with men and women on the stairs
And watched the tall white footman take the
    names,

And heard him shout them out, and there I
  shaped
My own name ready for him, "Mr. Brown."
And Mrs. Philby Phipp, hearing the name,
Would, I imagined, brighten suddenly
And smile and say, "How are you, Mr. Brown?"
And in an instant I'd remember her,
And where we met, and who was Mr. Phipp,
And all the jolly time at Grindelwald
(If that was where it was); and she and I
Would talk of Art and Politics and things
As we had talked these many years ago . . .
So "Mr. Brown" I murmured to the man,
And he — the fool! — he took a mighty breath
And shouted, "Mr. BROWNIE!" — Brownie!
  Yes,
He shouted "Mr. BROWNIE" to the roof.
And Mrs. Philby Phipp, hearing the name,
Brightened up suddenly and smiled and said,
"How are you, Mr. Brownie?" — (Brownie!
  Lord!)
And, while my mouth was open to protest,
"How do you do?" to some one at the back.
So I was passed along into the crowd
As Brownie!

Who on earth is Mr. Brownie?
Did he, I wonder, he and Mrs. Phipp
Talk Art and Politics at Grindelwald,
Or did one simply point him out to her
With "That is Mr. Brownie?" Were they friends,

Dear friends, or casual acquaintances?
She brightened at his name, some memory
Came back to her that brought a happy smile —
Why
surely they were friends! But *I* am Brown,
A stranger, all unknown to Mrs. Phipp,
As she to me, a common interloper — I
see it now — an uninvited guest,
Whose card was clearly meant for Mr. Brownie.
Soft music fell, and the kaleidoscope
Of lovely woman glided, swayed and turned
Beneath the shaded lights; but Mr. Brownie
(Né Brown, not Brownie) stood upon one side
And brooded silently. Some spoke to him;
Whether to Brown or Brownie mattered not,
He did not answer, did not notice them,
Just stood and brooded . . . Then went home to
    bed.

A Few Tricks For Christmas

(In the manner of many contemporaries)

Now that the "festive season" (copyright) is approaching, it behooves us all to prepare ourselves in some way to contribute to the gaiety of the Christmas house-party. A clever conjurer is welcome anywhere, and those of us whose powers of entertainment are limited to the setting of booby-traps or the arranging of apple-pie beds must view with envy the much greater tribute of laughter and applause which is the lot of the prestidigitator with some natural gift for legerdemain. Fortunately there are a few simple conjuring tricks which are within the reach of us all. With practice even the clumsiest of us can obtain sufficient dexterity in the art of illusion to puzzle the most observant of our fellow-guests. The few simple tricks which I am about to explain, if studied diligently for a few days before Christmas, will make a genuine addition to the gaiety of any gathering, and the amateur prestidigitator (if I may use that word again) will find that he is amply repaying the hospitality of his host and hostess by his contribution to the general festivity.

So much by way of introduction. It is a difficult style of writing to keep up, particularly when the number of synonyms for "conjuring" is so strictly limited. Let me now get to the tricks. I call the first

HOLDING THE LEMON

For this trick you want a lemon and a pack of ordinary playing-cards. Cutting the lemon in two, you hand half to one member of your audience and half to another, asking them to hold the halves up in full view of the company. Then, taking the pack of cards in your own hands, you offer it to a third member of the party, requesting him to select a card and examine it carefully. When he has done this he puts it back in the pack, and you seize this opportunity to look hurriedly at the face of it, discovering (let us say) that it is the five of spades. Once more you shuffle the pack; and then, going through the cards one by one, you will have no difficulty in locating the five of spades, which you will hold up to the company with the words "I think this is your card, sir" — whereupon the audience will testify by its surprise and appreciation that you have guessed correctly.

It will be noticed that, strictly speaking, the lemon is not a necessary adjunct of this trick; but the employment of it certainly adds an air of mystery to the initial stages of the illusion, and this air of mystery is, after all, the chief stock-in-trade of the successful conjurer.

For my next trick, which I call

THE ILLUSORY EGG

and which is most complicated, you require a sponge, two tablecloths, a handful of nuts, a rabbit, five yards of coloured ribbon, a top-hat with a hole in it, a hard-boiled egg, two florins and a gentleman's watch. Having obtained all these things, which may take some time, you put the two tablecloths aside and separate the other articles into two heaps, the rabbit, the top-hat, the hard-boiled egg, and the handful of nuts being in one heap, and the ribbon, the sponge, the gentleman's watch and the two florins in the other. This being done, you cover each heap with a tablecloth, so that none of the objects beneath is in any way visible. Then you invite any gentleman in the audience to think of a number. Let us suppose he thinks of 38. In that case you ask any lady in the audience to think of an odd number, and she suggests (shall we say?) 29. Then, asking the company to watch you carefully, you — you — To tell the truth, I have forgotten just what it is you *do* do, but I know that it is a very good trick, and never fails to create laughter and bewilderment. It is distinctly an illusion worth trying, and, if you begin it in the manner I have described, quite possibly some way of finishing it up will occur to you on the spur of the moment. By multiplying the two numbers together and passing the hard-boiled egg through the sponge and then taking the . . . or is it the — Anyway, I'm certain you have to have a piece of elastic up the sleeve . . . and

I know one of the florins has to — No, it's no good, I can't remember it.

But mention of the two numbers reminds me of a trick which I haven't forgotten. It is a thought-reading illusion, and always creates the *maximum* of wonderment amongst the audience. It is called

THE THREE QUESTIONS

As before, you ask a gentleman in the company to write down a number on a piece of paper, and a lady to write down another number. These numbers they show to the other guests. You then inform the company that you will ask any one of them three questions, and by the way they are answered you will guess what the product of the two numbers is. (For instance, if the numbers were 13 and 17, then 13 multiplied by 17 is — let's see, thirteen sevens are — thirteen sevens — seven threes are twenty-one, seven times one is — well, look here, let's suppose the numbers are 10 and 17. Then the product is 170, and 170 is the number you have got to guess.)

Well, the company selects a lady to answer your questions, and the first thing you ask her is: "When was Magna Charta signed?" Probably she says that she doesn't know. Then you say, "What is the capital of Persia?" She answers Timbuctoo, or Omar Khayyam, according to how well informed she is. Then comes your last question: "What makes lightning?" She is practically certain to say, "Oh, the thunder." Then you

209

tell her that the two numbers multiplied together come to 170.

How is this remarkable trick performed? It is quite simple. The two people whom you asked to think of the numbers are confederates, and you arranged with them beforehand that they should write down 10 and 17. Of course it would be a much better trick if they weren't confederates; but in that case I don't quite know how you would do it.

I shall end up this interesting and instructive article with a rather more difficult illusion. For the tricks I have already explained it was sufficient that the amateur prestidigitator (I shall only say this once more) should know how it was done; for my last trick he will also require a certain aptitude for legerdemain in order to do it. But a week's quiet practice at home will give him all the skill that is necessary.

THE MYSTERIOUS PUDDING

is one of the oldest and most popular illusions. You begin by borrowing a gold watch from one of your audience. Having removed the works, you wrap the empty case up in a handkerchief and hand it back to him, asking him to put it in his waistcoat pocket. The works you place in an ordinary pudding basin and proceed to pound up with a hammer. Having reduced them to powder, you cover the basin with another handkerchief, which you borrow from a member of the company, and announce that you are about to make a plum-pudding. Cutting a small hole in the top of the

210

handkerchief, you drop a lighted match through the aperture; whereupon the handkerchief flares up. When the flames have died down you exhibit the basin, wherein (to the surprise of all) is to be seen an excellent Christmas pudding, which you may ask your audience to sample. At the same time you tell the owner of the watch that if he feels in his pockets he will find his property restored to him intact; and to his amazement he discovers that the works in some mysterious way have got back into his watch, and that the handkerchief in which it was wrapped up has gone!

Now for the explanation of this ingenious illusion. The secret of it is that you have a second basin, with a pudding in it, concealed in the palm of your right hand. At the critical moment, when the handkerchief flares up, you take advantage of the excitement produced to substitute the one basin for the other. The watch from which you extract the works is not the borrowed one, but one which you have had concealed between the third and fourth fingers of the left hand. You show the empty case of this watch to the company, before wrapping the watch in the handkerchief and handing it back to its owner. Meanwhile with the aid of a little wax you have attached an invisible hair to the handkerchief, the other end of it being fastened to the palm of your left hand. With a little practice it is not difficult to withdraw the handkerchief, by a series of trifling jerks, from, the pocket of your fellow-guest to its resting place between the first and second finger of your left hand.

One word more. I am afraid that the borrowed handkerchief to which you applied the match really did get burnt, and you will probably have to offer the owner one of your own instead. That is the only weak spot in one of the most baffling tricks ever practised by the amateur prestidigitator (to use the word for the last time). It will make a fitting climax to your evening's entertainment — an entertainment which will ensure you another warm invitation next year when the "festive season" (*copyright*) comes upon us once again.

And Others

My Film Scenario

[Specially written for Economic Pictures, Limited, whose Manager has had the good fortune to pick up for a mere song (or, to be more accurate, for a few notes) several thousand miles of discarded cinema films from a bankrupt company. The films comprise the well-known "Baresark Basil, the Pride of the Ranch" (two miles long), "The Foiler Foiled" (one mile, three furlongs, two rods, poles or perches), "The Blood-stained Vest" (fragment — eighteen inches), "A Maniac's Revenge" (5,000 feet), "The Life of the Common Mosquito" (six legs), and so forth.]

Twenty-five years before our film opens, Andrew Bellingham, a young man just about to enter his father's business, was spending a holiday in a little fishing village in Cornwall. The daughter of the sheep-farmer with whom he lodged was a girl of singular beauty, and Andrew's youthful blood was quickly stirred to admiration. Carried away by his passion for her, he —

[MANAGER. *Just a reminder that Mr. T.P. O'Connor has to pass this before it can be produced.*]
— he married her —

[MANAGER. *Oh, I beg pardon.*] — and for some weeks they lived happily together. One day he informed Jessie that he would have to go back to his work in London, and that it might be a year or more before he could acknowledge her openly as his wife to his rich and proud parents. Jessie was prostrated with grief; and late that afternoon her hat and fringe-net were discovered by the edge of the waters. Realizing at once that she must have drowned herself in her distress, Andrew took an affecting farewell of her father and the sheep, and returned to London. A year later he married a distant cousin, and soon rose to a condition of prosperity. At the time our film begins to unwind, he was respected by everybody in the City, a widower, and the father of a beautiful girl of eighteen called Hyacinth.

[MANAGER. *Now we're off. What do we start with?*]

I

On the sunny side of Fenchurch Street —

[MANAGER. *Ah, then I suppose we'd better keep back the Rescue from the Alligator and the Plunge down Niagara in a Barrel.*]

— Andrew Bellingham was dozing in his office. Suddenly he awoke to find a strange man standing over him.

"Who are you?" asked Mr. Bellingham. "What do you want?"

216

"My name is Jasper," was the answer, "and I have some information to give you." He bent down and hissed, "*Your first wife is still alive!*"

Andrew started up in obvious horror. "My daughter," he gasped, "my little Hyacinth! She must never know."

"Listen. Your wife is in Spain —

[MANAGER. *Don't waste her. Make it somewhere where there are sharks.*

AUTHOR. *It's all right, she's dead really.*] — and she will not trouble you. Give me a thousand pounds and you shall have these; and he held out a packet containing the marriage certificate, a photograph of Jessie's father dipping a sheep, a receipted bill for a pair of white gloves, size 9-1/2, two letters signed 'Your own loving little Andy Pandy,' and a peppermint with 'Jess' on it in pink. Once these are locked up in your safe, no one need ever know that you were married in Cornwall twenty-five years ago."

Without a moment's hesitation Mr. Bellingham took a handful of bank notes from his pocketbook, and the exchange was made. At all costs he must preserve his little Hyacinth from shame. Now she need never know. With a forced smile he bowed Jasper out, placed the packet in his safe and returned to his desk.

But his mysterious visitor was not done with yet. As soon as the door had closed behind him Jasper re-entered softly, drugged Andrew hastily, and took possession again of the compromising documents. By the time Mr. Bellingham had regained his senses the thief was away. A hue-and-cry was raised, police whistles were blown, and Richard Harrington, Mr. Bellingham's private secretary, was smartly arrested.

At the trial things looked black against Richard. He was poor and he was in love with Hyacinth; the chain of evidence was complete. In spite of his impassioned protest from the dock, in spite of Hyacinth's dramatic swoon in front of the solicitor's table, the judge with great solemnity passed sentence of twenty years' penal servitude. A loud "Hear, hear" from the gallery rang through the court, and, looking up, Mr. Bellingham caught the sardonic eye of the mysterious Jasper.

II

Richard had been in prison a month before the opportunity for his escape occurred. For a month he had been hewing stone in Portland, black despair at his heart. Then, like lightning, he saw his chance and took it. The warders were off guard for a moment. Hastily lifting his pickaxe —

[MANAGER. *Sorry, but it's a spade in the only prison film we've got.*]

Hastily borrowing a spade from a comrade who was digging potatoes, he struck several of his gaolers down, and, dodging the shots of others who hurried to the scene, he climbed the prison wall and dashed for freedom.

Reaching Weymouth at nightfall, he made his way to the house which Hyacinth had taken in order to be near him, and, suitably disguised, travelled up to London with her in the powerful motor which she had kept ready. "At last, my love, we are together," he murmured as they neared Wimbledon. But he had spoken a moment too soon. An aeroplane swooped down upon them, and Hyacinth was snatched from his arms and disappeared with her captors into the clouds.

III

Richard's first act on arriving in London was to go to Mr. Bellingham's house. Andrew was out, but a note lying on his study carpet, "*Meet me at the Old Windmill to-night*," gave him a clue. On receipt of this note Andrew had gone to the rendezvous, and it was no surprise to him when Jasper stepped out and offered to sell him a packet containing a marriage certificate, a photograph of an old gentleman dipping a sheep, a peppermint lozenge with "Jess" on it, and various other documents for a thousand pounds.

"You villain," cried Andrew, "even at the trial I suspected you," and he rushed at him fiercely.

A desperate struggle ensued. Breaking free for a moment from the vice-like grip of the other, Jasper leapt with the spring of a panther at one of the sails of the windmill as it came round, and was whirled upwards; with the spring of another panther, Andrew leapt on to the next sail and was whirled after him. At that moment the wind dropped, and the combatants were suspended in mid-air.

It was upon this terrible scene that Richard arrived. Already a crowd was collecting; and, though at present it did not seem greatly alarmed, feeling convinced that it was only assisting at another cinematograph rehearsal, its suspicions might at any moment be aroused. With a shout he dashed into the mill. Seeing him coming Jasper dropped his revolver and slid down the sail into the window. In a moment he reappeared at the door of the mill with Hyacinth under his arm. "Stop him!" cried Richard from underneath a sack of flour. It was no good. Jasper had leapt with his fair burden upon the back of his mustang and was gone . . .

The usual pursuit followed.

IV

It was the gala night at the Royal Circus. Ricardo Harringtoni, the wonderful new acrobat of whom everybody was talking, stood high above the crowd on his platform. His marvellous performance on the swinging horizontal bar was about to begin. Richard Harrington (for it was he) was troubled. Since he had entered on his new profession — as a disguise from the police who were still searching for him — he had had a vague suspicion that the lion-tamer was dogging him. *Who was the lion-tamer?* Could it be Jasper?

At that moment the band struck up and Richard leapt lightly on to the swinging bar. With a movement full of grace he let go of the bar and swung on to the opposite platform. And then, even as he was in mid-air, he realized what was happening.

Jasper had let the lion loose!

It was waiting for him.

With a gasping cry Ricardo Harringtoni fainted.

V

When he recovered consciousness, Richard found himself on the S.S. "Boracic," which was forging her way through the —

[MANAGER. *Somewhere where there are sharks.*]

— the Indian Ocean. Mr. Bellingham was bathing his forehead with cooling drinks.

"Forgive me, my boy," said Mr. Bellingham, "for the wrong I did you. It was Jasper who stole the compromising documents. He refuses to give them back unless I let him marry Hyacinth. What can I do?"

"Where is she?" asked Richard.

"Hidden away no one knows where. Find her, get back the documents for me, and she is yours."

At that moment a terrible cry rang through the ship, "Man overboard!" Pushing over Mr. Bellingham and running on deck, Richard saw that a woman and her baby were battling for life in the shark-infested waters. In an instant he had plunged in and rescued them. As they were dragged together up the ship's side he heard her murmur, "Is little Jasper safe?"

"Jasper?" cried Richard.

"Yes, called after his daddy."

"Where is daddy now?" asked Richard hoarsely.

"In America."

"Can't you see the likeness?" whispered Richard to Mr. Bellingham. "It must be. The villain is married to another. But now I will pursue him and get back the papers." And he left the boat at the next port and boarded one for America.

The search through North and South America for Jasper was protracted. Accompanied sometimes by a band of cowboys, sometimes by a tribe of Indians, Richard scoured the continent for his enemy. There were hours when he would rest awhile and amuse himself by watching the antics of the common mosquito [Manager. *Good!*] or he would lie at full length and gaze at a bud bursting into flower. [Manager. *Excellent!*] Then he would leap on to his steed and pursue the trail relentlessly once more.

One night he was dozing by his camp-fire, when he was awakened roughly by strong arms around his neck and Jasper's hot breath in his ear.

"At last!" cried Jasper, and, knocking Richard heavily on the head with a boot, he picked up his unconscious enemy and carried him to a tributary of the Amazon noted for its alligators. Once there he tied him to a post in mid-stream and rode hastily off to the nearest town, where he spent the evening witnessing the first half of "The Merchant of Venice." [Manager. *Splendid!*] But in the morning a surprise awaited him. As he was proceeding along the top of a lonely cliff he was confronted suddenly by the enemy whom he had thought to kill.

"Richard!" he cried, "escaped again!"

"Now, Jasper, I have you."

With a triumphant cry they rushed at each other; a terrible contest ensued; and then Jasper, with one blow of his palm, hurled his adversary over the precipice.

222

VI

How many times the two made an end of each other after this the pictures will show. Sometimes Jasper sealed Richard in a barrel and pushed him over Niagara; sometimes Richard tied Jasper to a stake and set light to him; sometimes they would both fall out of a balloon together. But the day of reckoning was at hand.

[Manager. *We've only got the Burning House and the 1913 Derby left.*

Author. *Right.*]

It is the evening of the 3rd of June. A cry rends the air suddenly, whistles are blowing, there is a rattling of horses' hoofs. "Fire! Fire!" Richard, who was passing Soho Square at the time, heard the cry and dashed into the burning house. In a room full of smoke he perceived a cowering woman. Hyacinth! To pick her up was the work of a moment, but how shall he save her? Stay! The telegraph wire! His training at the Royal Circus stood him in good stead. Treading lightly on the swaying wire he carried Hyacinth across to the house opposite.

"At last, my love," he breathed.

"But the papers," she cried. "You must get them, or father will not let you marry me."

Once more he treads the rocking wire; once more he re-crosses, with the papers on his back. Then the house behind him crumbles to the ground, with the wicked Jasper in its ruins . . .

"Excellent," said Mr. Bellingham at dinner that evening. "Not only are the papers here, but a full confession by Jasper. My first wife was drowned all the time; he stole the documents from her father. Richard, my boy, when the Home Secretary knows everything he will give you a free pardon. And then you can marry my daughter."

At these words Hyacinth and Richard were locked in a close embrace. On the next day they all went to the Derby together.

The Fatal Gift

People say to me sometimes, "Oh, *you* know Woolman, don't you?" I acknowledge that I do, and, after the silence that always ensues, I add, "If you want to say anything against him, please go on." You can almost hear the sigh of relief that goes up. "I thought he was a friend of yours," they say cheerfully. "But, of course, if —" and then they begin.

I think it is time I explained my supposed friendship for Ernest Merrowby Woolman — confound him.

The affair began in a taxicab two years ago. Andrew had been dining with me that night; we walked out to the cab-rank together; I told the driver where to go, and Andrew stepped in, waved good-bye to me from the window, and sat down suddenly upon something hard. He drew it from beneath him, and found it was an extremely massive (and quite new) silver cigar-case. He put it in his pocket with the intention of giving it to the driver when he got out, but quite naturally forgot. Next morning he found it on his dressing-table. So he put it in his pocket again, meaning to leave it at Scotland Yard on his way to the City.

Next morning it was on his dressing-table again.

This went on for some days. After a week or so Andrew saw that it was hopeless to try to get a cigar-case back to Scotland Yard in this casual sort of way; it must be taken there deliberately by somebody who had a morning to spare and was willing to devote it to this special purpose. He placed the case, therefore, prominently on a small table in the dining-room to await the occasion; calling also the attention of his family to it, as an excuse for an outing when they were not otherwise engaged.

At times he used to say, "I must really take that cigar-case to Scotland Yard to-morrow."

At other times he would say, "Somebody must really take that cigar-case to Scotland Yard to-day."

And so the weeks rolled on . . .

It was about a year later that I first got mixed up with the thing. I must have dined with the Andrews several times without noticing the cigar-case, but on this occasion it caught my eye as we wandered out to join the ladies, and I picked it up carelessly. Well, not exactly carelessly; it was too heavy for that.

"Why didn't you tell me," I said, "that you had stood for Parliament and that your supporters had consoled you with a large piece of plate? Hallo, they've put the wrong initials on it. How unbusiness-like."

"Oh, *that*?" said Andrew. "Is it still there?"

"Why not? It's quite a solid little table. But you haven't explained why your constituents, who must have seen your name on hundreds of posters, thought your initials were E.M.W."

Andrew explained.

"Then it isn't yours at all?" I said in amazement.

"Of course not."

"But, my dear man, this is theft. Stealing by finding, they call it. You could get" — I looked at him almost with admiration — "you could get two years for this"; and I weighed the cigar-case in my hand. "I believe you're the only one of my friends who could be certain of two years," I went on musingly. "Let's see, there's —"

"Nonsense," said Andrew uneasily. "But still, perhaps I'd better take it back to Scotland Yard tomorrow."

"And tell them you've kept it for a year? They'd run you in at once. No, what you want to do is to get rid of it without their knowledge. But how — that's the question. You can't give it away because of the initials."

"It's easy enough. I can leave it in another cab, or drop it in the river."

"Andrew, Andrew," I cried, "you're determined to go to prison! Don't you know from all the humorous articles you've ever read that, if you *try* to lose anything, then you never can? It's one of the stock remarks one makes to women in the endeavour to keep them amused. No, you must think of some more subtle way of disposing of it."

"I'll pretend it's yours," said Andrew more subtly, and he placed it in my pocket.

"No, you don't," I said. "But I tell you what I will do. I'll take it for a week and see if I can get rid of it. If I can't, I shall give it you back and wash my hands of the whole business — except, of course, for the monthly letter or whatever it is they allow you at the Scrubbs. You may still count on me for that."

And then the extraordinary thing happened. The next morning I received a letter from a stranger, asking for some simple information which I could have given him on a post-card. And so I should have done — or possibly, I am afraid, have forgotten to answer at all — but for the way that the letter ended up.

"Yours very truly,

ERNEST M. WOOLMAN."

The magic initials! It was a chance not to be missed. I wrote enthusiastically back and asked him to lunch.

He came. I gave him all the information he wanted, and more. Whether he was a pleasant sort of person or not I hardly noticed; I was so very pleasant myself.

He returned my enthusiasm. He asked me to dine with him the following week. A little party at the Savoy — his birthday, you know.

I accepted gladly. I rolled up at the party with my little present . . . a massive silver cigar-case . . . suitably engraved.

So there you are. He clings to me. He seems to have formed the absurd idea that I am fond of him. A few months after that evening at the Savoy he was married. I was invited to the wedding — confound him. Of course I had to live up to my birthday present; the least I could do was an enormous silver cigar-box (not engraved), which bound me to him still more strongly.

By that time I realized that I hated him. He was pushing, familiar, everything that I disliked. All my friends wondered how I had become so intimate with him . . .

Well, now they know. And the original E.M.W., if he has the sense to read this, also knows. If he cares to prosecute Ernest Merrowby Woolman for being in possession of stolen goods, I shall be glad to give him any information. Woolman is generally to be found leaving my rooms at about 6.30 in the evening, and a smart detective could easily nab him as he steps out.

To The Death

(In the Twentieth Century manner)

"Cauliflower!" shrieked Gaspard Volauvent across the little table in the *estaminet*. His face bristled with rage.

"Serpent!" replied Jacques Rissole, bristling with equal dexterity.

The two stout little men glared ferociously at each other. Then Jacques picked up his glass and poured the wine of the country over his friend's head.

"Drown, serpent!" he said magnificently. He beckoned to the waiter. "Another bottle," he said. "My friend has drunk all this."

Gaspard removed the wine from his whiskers with the local paper and leant over the table towards Jacques.

"This must be wiped out in blood," he said slowly. "You understand?"

"Perfectly," replied the other. "The only question is whose."

"Name your weapons," said Gaspard Volauvent grandly.

"Aeroplanes," replied Jacques Rissole after a moment's thought.

"Bah! I cannot fly."

"Then I win," said Jacques simply.

230

The other looked at him in astonishment.

"What! You fly?"

"No; but I can learn."

"Then I will learn too," said Gaspard with dignity. "We meet — in six months?"

"Good." Jacques pointed to the ceiling. "Say three thousand feet up."

"Three thousand four hundred," said Gaspard for the sake of disagreeing.

"After all, that is for our seconds to arrange. My friend Epinard of the Roullens Aerodrome will act for me. He will also instruct me how to bring serpents to the ground."

"With the idea of cleansing the sky of cauliflowers," said Gaspard, "I shall proceed to the flying-ground at Dormancourt; Blanchaille, the instructor there, will receive your friend."

He bowed and walked out.

Details were soon settled. On a date six months ahead the two combatants would meet three thousand two hundred feet above the little town in which they lived, and fight to the death. In the event of both crashing, the one who crashed last would be deemed the victor. It was Gaspard's second who insisted on this clause; Gaspard himself felt that it did not matter greatly.

The first month of instruction went by. At the end of it Jacques Rissole had only one hope. It was that when he crashed he should crash on some of Gaspard's family. Gaspard had no hope, but one consolation. It was that no crash could involve his stomach, which he invariably left behind him as soon as the aeroplane rose.

At the end of the second month Gaspard wrote to Jacques.

"My friend," he wrote, "the hatred of you which I nurse in my bosom, and which fills me with the desire to purge you from the sky, is in danger of being transferred to my instructor. Let us therefore meet and renew our enmity."

Jacques Rissole wrote back to Gaspard.

"My enemy," he wrote, "there is nobody in the whole of the Roullens Aerodrome whom I do not detest with a detestation beside which my hatred for you seems as maudlin adoration. This is notwithstanding the fact that I make the most marvellous progress in the art of flying. It is merely something in their faces which annoys me. Let me therefore see yours again, in the hope that it will make me think more kindly of theirs."

They met, poured wine over each other and parted. After another month the need of a further stimulant was felt. They met again, and agreed to insult each other weekly.

On the last day of his training Gaspard spoke seriously to his instructor.

"You see that I make nothing of it," he said. "My thoughts are ever with the stomach that I leave behind. Not once have I been in a position to take control. How then can I fight? My friend, I arrange it all. You shall take my place."

"Is that quite fair to Rissole?" asked Blanchaille doubtfully.

"Do not think that I want you to hurt him. That is not necessary. He will hurt himself. Keep out of his way until he has finished with himself, and then fly back here. It is easy."

It seemed the best way; indeed the only way. Gaspard Volauvent could never get to the rendezvous alone, and it would be fatal to his honour if Jacques arrived there and found nobody to meet him. Reluctantly Blanchaille agreed.

At the appointed hour Gaspard put his head cautiously out of his bedroom window and gazed up into the heavens. He saw two aeroplanes straight above him. At the thought that he might have been in one of them he shuddered violently. Indeed, he felt so unwell that the need for some slight restorative became pressing. He tripped off to the *estaminet*.

It was empty save for one table. Gaspard walked towards it, hoping for a little conversation. The occupant lowered the newspaper from in front of his face and looked up.

It was too much for Gaspard.

"Coward!" he shrieked.

Jacques, who had been going to say the same thing, hastily substituted "Serpent!"

"I know you," cried Gaspard. "You send your instructor up in your place. Poltroon!"

Jacques picked up his glass and poured the wine of the country over his friend's head.

"Drown, serpent," he said magnificently. He beckoned to the waiter. "Another bottle," he said. "My friend has drunk all this."

Gaspard removed the wine from his whiskers with Jacques' paper, and leant over him.

"This must be wiped out in blood," he said slowly. "Name your weapons."

"Submarines," said Jacques after a moment's thought.

The Legend Of Hi-you

I

In the days of Good King Carraway (dead now, poor
fellow, but he had a pleasant time while he lasted) there
lived a certain swineherd commonly called Hi-You. It
was the duty of Hi-You to bring up one hundred and
forty-one pigs for his master, and this he did with as
much enthusiasm as the work permitted. But there
were times when his profession failed him. In the blue
days of summer Princes and Princesses, Lords and
Ladies, Chamberlains and Enchanters would ride past
him and leave him vaguely dissatisfied with his
company, so that he would remove the straw from his
mouth and gaze after them, wondering what it would
be like to have as little regard for a swineherd as they.
But when they were out of sight, he would replace the
straw in his mouth and fall with great diligence to the
counting of his herd and such other duties as are
required of the expert pigtender, assuring himself that,
if a man could not be lively with one hundred and
forty-one companions, he must indeed be a poor-
spirited sort of fellow.

Now there was one little black pig for whom Hi-You
had a special tenderness. Just so, he often used to think,
would he have felt towards a brother if this had been

granted to him. It was not the colour of the little pig nor the curliness of his tail (endearing though this was), nor even the melting expression in his eyes which warmed the swineherd's heart, but the feeling that intellectually this pig was as solitary among the hundred and forty others as Hi-You himself. Frederick (for this was the name which he had given to it) shared their food, their sleeping apartments, much indeed as did Hi-You, but he lived, or so it seemed to the other, an inner life of his own. In short, Frederick was a soulful pig.

There could be only one reason for this: Frederick was a Prince in disguise. Some enchanter — it was a common enough happening in those days — annoyed by Frederick's father, or his uncle, or even by Frederick himself, had turned him into a small black pig until such time as the feeling between them had passed away. There was a Prince Frederick of Milvania who had disappeared suddenly; probably this was he. His complexion was darker now, his tail more curly, but the royal bearing was unmistakable.

It was natural then that, having little in common with his other hundred and forty charges, Hi-You should find himself drawn into ever closer companionship with Frederick. They would talk together in the intervals of acorn-hunting, Frederick's share of the conversation limited to "Humphs," unintelligible at first, but, as the days went on, seeming more and more charged with an inner meaning to Hi-You, until at last he could interpret every variation of grunt with which his small black friend responded. And indeed it was a pretty sight to see them sitting together on the top of a hill, the world at their feet, discussing at one time the political situation of Milvania, at another the latest ballad of the countryside, or even in their more hopeful moments planning what they should do when Frederick at last was restored to public life.

II

Now it chanced that one morning when Frederick and Hi-You were arguing together in a friendly manner over the new uniforms of the Town Guard (to the colours of which Frederick took exception) King Carraway himself passed that way, and being in a good humour stood for a moment listening to them.

"Well, well," he said at last, "well, well, well."

In great surprise Hi-You looked up, and then, seeing that it was the King, jumped to his feet and bowed several times.

"Pardon, Your Majesty," he stammered, "I did not see Your Majesty. I was — I was talking."

"To a pig," laughed the King.

"To His Royal Highness Prince Frederick of Milvania," said Hi-You proudly.

"I beg your pardon," said the King; "could I trouble you to say that again?"

"His Royal Highness Prince Frederick of Milvania."

"Yes, that was what it sounded like last time."

"Frederick," murmured Hi-You in his friend's ear, "this is His Majesty King Carraway. He lets me call him Frederick," he added to the King.

"You don't mean to tell me," said His Majesty, pointing to the pig, "that *this* is Prince Frederick?"

"It is indeed, Sire. Such distressing incidents must often have occurred within Your Majesty's recollection."

"They have, yes. Dear me, dear me."

"Humph," remarked Frederick, feeling it was time he said something.

"His Royal Highness says that he is very proud to meet so distinguished a monarch as Your Majesty."

"Did he say that?" asked the King, surprised.

"Undoubtedly, Your Majesty."

"Very good of him, I'm sure."

"Humph," said Frederick again.

"He adds," explained Hi-You, "that Your Majesty's great valour is only excelled by the distinction of Your Majesty's appearance."

"Dear me," said the King, "I thought he was merely repeating himself. It seems to me very clever of you to understand so exactly what he is saying."

"Humph," said Frederick, feeling that it was about acorn time again.

"His Royal Highness is kind enough to say that we are very old friends."

"Yes, of course, that must make a difference. One soon picks it up, no doubt. But we must not be inhospitable to so distinguished a visitor. Certainly he must stay with us at the Palace. And you had better come along too, my man, for it may well be that without your aid some of His Royal Highness's conversation would escape us. Prince Frederick of

Milvania — dear me, dear me. This will be news for Her Royal Highness."

So, leaving the rest of the herd to look after itself, as it was quite capable of doing, Frederick and Hi-You went to the Palace.

Now Her Royal Highness Princess Amaril was of an age to be married. Many Princes had sought her hand, but in vain, for she was as proud as she was beautiful. Indeed, her beauty was so great that those who looked upon it were blinded, as if they had gazed upon the sun at noonday — or so the Court Poet said, and he would not be likely to exaggerate. Wherefore Hi-You was filled with a great apprehension as he walked to the Palace, and Frederick, to whom the matter had been explained, was, it may be presumed, equally stirred within, although outwardly impassive. And, as they went, Hi-You murmured to his companion that it was quite all right, for that in any event she could not eat them, the which assurance Frederick, no doubt, was peculiarly glad to receive.

"Ah," said the King, as they were shown into the Royal Library, "that's right." He turned to the Princess. "My dear, prepare for a surprise."

"Yes, Father," said Amaril dutifully.

"This," said His Majesty dramatically, throwing out a hand, "is a Prince in disguise."

"Which one, Father?" said Amaril.

"The small black one, of course," said the King crossly; "the other is merely his attendant. Hi, you, what's your name?"

The swineherd hastened to explain that His Majesty, with His Majesty's unfailing memory for names, had graciously mentioned it.

"You don't say anything," said the King to his daughter.

Princess Amaril sighed.

"He is very handsome, Father," she said, looking at Hi-You.

"Y-yes," said the King, regarding Frederick (who was combing himself thoughtfully behind the left ear) with considerable doubt. "But the real beauty of Prince Frederick's character does not lie upon the surface, or anyhow — er — not at the moment."

"No, Father," sighed Amaril, and she looked at Hi-You again.

Now the swineherd, who with instinctive good breeding had taken the straw from his mouth on entering the Palace, was a well-set-up young fellow, such as might please even a Princess.

For a little while there was silence in the Royal Library, until Frederick realized that it was his turn to speak.

"Humph!" said Frederick.

"There!" said the King in great good humour. "Now, my dear, let me tell you what that means. That means that His Royal Highness is delighted to meet so beautiful and distinguished a Princess." He turned to Hi-You. "Isn't that right, my man?"

"Perfectly correct, Your Majesty."

"You see, my dear," said the King complacently, "one soon picks it up. Now in a few days —"

"Humph!" said Frederick again.

"What did that one mean, Father?" asked Amaril.

"That meant — er — that meant — well, it's a little hard to put it colloquially, but roughly it means" — he made a gesture with his hand — "that we have — er — been having very charming weather lately." He frowned vigorously at the swineherd.

"Exactly, Your Majesty," said Hi-You.

"Charming weather for the time of year."

"For the time of year, of course," said the King hastily. "One naturally assumes that. Well, my dear," he went on to his daughter, "I'm sure you will be glad to know that Prince Frederick has consented to stay with us for a little. You will give orders that suitable apartments are to be prepared."

"Yes, Father. What *are* suitable apartments?"

The King pulled at his beard and regarded Frederick doubtfully.

"Perhaps it would be better," the Princess went on, looking at Hi-You, "if this gentleman —"

"Of course, my dear, of course. Naturally His Royal Highness would wish to retain his suite."

"Humph!" said Frederick, meaning, I imagine, that things were looking up.

III

Of all the Princes who from time to time had visited the Court none endeared himself so rapidly to the people as did Frederick of Milvania. His complete lack of vanity, his thoughtfulness, the intense reserve which so obviously indicated a strong character, his power of listening placidly to even the most tedious of local dignitaries, all these were virtues of which previous royal visitors had given no sign. Moreover on set occasions Prince Frederick could make a very pretty speech. True, this was read for him, owing to a slight affection of the throat from which, as the Chancellor pointed out, His Royal Highness was temporarily suffering, but it would be couched in the most perfect taste and seasoned at suitable functions (such, for instance, as the opening of the first Public Baths) with a pleasantly restrained humour. Nor was there any doubt that the words were indeed the Prince's own, as dictated to Hi-You and by him put on paper for the Chancellor. But Hi-You himself never left the Palace.

"My dear," said the King to his daughter one day, "have you ever thought of marriage?"

"Often, Father," said Amaril.

"I understand from the Chancellor that the people are expecting an announcement on the subject shortly."

"We haven't got anything to announce, have we?"

"It's a pity that you were so hasty with your other suitors," said the King thoughtfully. "There is hardly a Prince left who is in any way eligible."

"Except Prince Frederick," said Amaril gently.

The King looked at her suspiciously and then looked away again, pulling at his beard.

"Of course," went on Amaril, "I don't know what your loving subjects would say about it."

"My loving subjects," said the King grimly, "have been properly brought up. They believe — they have my authority for believing — that they are suffering from a disability of the eyesight laid upon them by a wicked enchanter, under which they see Princes as — er — pigs. That, if you remember, was this fellow Hi-You's suggestion. And a very sensible one."

"But do you want Frederick as a son-in-law?"

"Well, that's the question. In his present shape he is perhaps not quite — not quite — well, how shall I put it?"

"Not quite," suggested Amaril.

"Exactly. At the same time I think that there could be no harm in the announcement of a betrothal. The marriage, of course, would not be announced until —"

"Until the enchanter had removed his spell from the eyes of the people?"

"Quite so. You have no objection to that, my dear?"

"I am His Majesty's subject," said Amaril dutifully.

"That's a good girl." He patted the top of her head and dismissed her.

So the betrothal of His Royal Highness Frederick of Milvania to the Princess Amaril was announced, to the great joy of the people. And in the depths of the Palace Hi-You the swineherd was hard at work compounding a potion which, he assured the King, would restore Frederick to his own princely form. And sometimes the Princess Amaril would help him at his work.

IV

A month went by, and then Hi-You came to the King with news. He had compounded the magic potion. A few drops sprinkled discriminately on Frederick would restore him to his earlier shape, and the wedding could then be announced.

"Well, my man," said His Majesty genially, "this is indeed pleasant hearing. We will sprinkle Frederick to-morrow. Really, I am very much in your debt; remind me after the ceremony to speak to the Lord Treasurer about the matter."

"Say no more," begged Hi-You. "All I ask is to be allowed to depart in peace. Let me have a few hours alone with His Royal Highness in the form in which I have known him so long, and then, when he is himself again, let me go. For it is not meet that I should remain here as a perpetual reminder to His Royal Highness of what he would fain forget."

"Well, that's very handsome of you, very handsome indeed. I see your point. Yes, it is better that you should go. But, before you go, there is just one thing. The people are under the impression that — er — an enchanter has — er — well, you remember what you yourself suggested."

"I have thought of that," said Hi-You, who seemed to have thought of everything. "And I venture to propose that Your Majesty should announce that a great alchemist has been compounding a potion to relieve their blindness. A few drops of this will be introduced into the water of the Public Baths, and all those bathing therein will be healed."

"A striking notion," said the King. "Indeed it was just about to occur to me. I will proclaim tomorrow a public holiday, and give orders that it be celebrated in

244

the baths. Then in the evening, when they are all clean — I should say 'cured' — we will present their Prince to them."

So it happened even as Hi-You had said, and in the evening the Prince, a model now of manly beauty, was presented to them, and they acclaimed him with cheers. And all noticed how lovingly the Princess regarded him, and how he smiled upon her.

But the King gazed upon the Prince as one fascinated. Seven times he cleared his throat and seven times he failed to speak. And the eighth time he said, "Your face is strangely familiar to me."

"Perchance we met in Milvania," said the Prince pleasantly.

Now the King had never been in Milvania. Wherefore he still gazed at the Prince, and at length he said, "What has happened to that Hi-You fellow?"

"You will never hear of him again," said the Prince pleasantly.

"Oh!" said the King. And after that they feasted

And some say that they feasted upon roast pig, but I say not. And some say that Hi-You had planned it all from the beginning, but I say not. And some say that it was the Princess Amaril who planned it, from the day when first she saw Hi-You, and with them I agree. For indeed I am very sure that when Hi-You was a swineherd upon the hills he believed truly that the little black pig with the curly tail was a Prince. And, though events in the end were too much for him, I like to think that Hi-You remained loyal to his friend, and that in his plush-lined sty in a quiet corner of the Palace grounds Frederick passed a gentle old age, cheered from time to time by the visits of Amaril's children.

Bless This House

Norah Lofts

The house was built in the Old Queen's time — built for an Elizabethan pirate who was knighted for the plunder he brought home. It survived many eras, many reigns — it saw the passing of Cromwell and the Civil War. It became rich with an Indian Nabob and poor with a twetieth century innkeeper. It saw wars, and lovers, and death. Children were born there, both heirs and bastards. It had ghosts and legends and a history that grew stranger with every generation.

The house was Merravay — and its story stretched over four hundred years . . .

ISBN 0-7531-7569-X (hb)
ISBN 0-7531-7570-3 (pb)

Death at the Dolphin

Ngaio Marsh

When the bombed-out Dolphin Theatre is given to Peregrine Jay by a wealthy but mysterious patron, he is overjoyed. And when the mysterious oil millionaire also gives him a glove that belonged to Shakespeare, Peregrine displays it in the dockside theatre and writes a successful play about it.

But then a murder takes place, a boy is attacked, and the glove is stolen. Could it be that oil and water don't mix? Inspector Roderick Alleyn is determined to find out . . .

ISBN 0-7531-7407-3 (hb)
ISBN 0-7531-7408-1 (pb)